Emmanuelle

Emmanuelle

EMMANUELLE ARSAN

Translated by

Lowell Bair

Grove Press
New York

Published simultaneously in Canada
Printed in the United States of America

ISBN: 978-0-8021-2235-3
eBook ISBN: 978-0-8021-9271-4

Grove Press
an imprint of Grove/Atlantic, Inc
154 West 14th Street
New York, NY 10011

Distributed by Publishers Group West
www.groveatlantic.com

To Jean

Or if the women you portray
Represent a wish of your fanciful senses . . .

—Stéphane Mallarmé
L'apres-midi d'un faune

Contents

Emmanuelle

We are not yet in the world
There is not yet a world
Things are not yet made
The reason for being is not found.

—Antonin Artaud

1

The Flying Unicorn

Love has a thousand postures; the simplest and the
least tiring is to lie halfway over on your right side.
—Ovid, *The Art of Love*

Emmanuelle boarded the plane in London that was to take her to Bangkok. At first the rich smell of leather, like that preserved in British cars after years of use, the otherworldly lighting, and the thickness and silence of the carpets were all she could grasp of the environment she was entering for the first time.

She did not understand what was being said to her by the smiling man who was guiding her, but she was not upset. Although her heart may have been beating faster, it was only from a sensation of strangeness, not from apprehension. The blue uniforms, the thoughtfulness and authority of the personnel assigned to welcome and initiate her—everything combined to create a feeling of security and euphoria. A new universe was going to be hers for the next twelve hours of her life, a universe with different laws, more constraining, but perhaps more delectable for that very reason. The vigilance of freedom was replaced by the leisure and placidity of subjection.

The steward led her to her seat. It was what would normally have been a window seat, but there was no window. She could see nothing beyond the draped walls. It made no difference to her. She did not care about anything but abandoning herself to the powers of that deep seat, drifting into drowsiness between its woolly arms, against its foam shoulder, on its long, mermaid lap.

An English stewardess stopped in the aisle. Her hands flew up to the rack above Emmanuelle's head to put away her light, leather traveling case. She spoke French and the impression of semi-torpor that Emmanuelle had been feeling for the past two days (she had arrived in London only the day before) was dispelled.

As the stewardess leaned over her, her blondeness made Emmanuelle's long hair seem still more nocturnal. They were both dressed nearly alike, but a brassiere showed through the English girl's blouse, while the slightest movement revealed that Emmanuelle's breasts were free under hers. She was glad that the stewardess was young and that her eyes were like her own—flecked with gold.

Emmanuelle tried to think of something to ask that would please her. Maybe she should show an interest in the plane. But before she could speak, two children—a boy and a girl— pushed aside the velvet curtain that separated Emmanuelle's row of seats from the row in front. They looked so much alike that one had to assume they were twins. Emmanuelle noted at a glance the graceless, conventional clothes that stamped them as English schoolchildren, their reddish blond hair, their expression of affected coldness, and the haughtiness with which they spat out brief words to the stewardess. Although they were apparently only twelve or thirteen, their confident manner created a distance between them and her that she had no thought of reducing. They sedately planted themselves in the two seats across the aisle from Emmanuelle. At the same time the last of the four passengers for whom the compartment was reserved came in and she turned her attention to him.

He was at least a head taller than she was. His hair and mustache were black. She liked his amber-colored suit. She judged him to be elegant and well-bred, two qualities that, after all, covered most of what one hoped to find in a fellow passenger. She tried to guess his age from the wrinkles at the corners of his eyes—forty, perhaps fifty? He would be more agreeable, she thought, than the two pretentious children.

The stewardess had left the compartment and, through the gap in the curtains, Emmanuelle could now see her blue hip pressed against an invisible passenger. She tried to turn her eyes away. Her black hair whipped her cheeks and flowed over her face. Then the English girl straightened up, turned toward the rear of the plane, appeared between the curtains, pushing their long legs apart with her hands, and stepped toward Emmanuelle. "Would you like me to introduce your traveling companions to you?" she asked; and, without waiting for an answer, she told her the man's name. Emmanuelle thought she heard "Eisenhower," which amused her and made her miss the names of the twins.

The man began talking to her in English. She had no idea what he was saying. Seeing her perplexity, the stewardess questioned the three others, then laughed, showing the tip of her tongue. "What a pity!" she said lightheartedly. "None of them knows a single word of French. This will be a good chance for you to brush up on your English!"

Before Emmanuelle could protest, the stewardess moved her fingers in a graceful, cryptic gesture to her passengers, turned on her heel, and walked away. Emmanuelle was again alone. She felt like sulking, holding herself aloof from everything.

A loudspeaker hidden behind the draperies came to life. After a male voice had spoken in English, Emmanuelle recognized the stewardess speaking in French ("For me," she thought), welcoming the passengers aboard the Flying Unicorn and giving flight instructions.

The awakening of the jet engines was indicated by a murmur and a slight quivering of the soundproof walls. Emmanuelle was not even aware that the plane was moving along the runway. And it was a long time before she realized that she was flying.

She did not realize it, in fact, until the red light went off and the man beside her stood up and offered, by gestures, to put away her jacket, which she had kept on her knees without knowing why. She let him take it. He smiled, opened a book, and stopped looking at her. A waiter appeared, carrying a tray of glasses. She chose a cocktail by its color, but it was not the one she expected; it was stronger.

What must have been an afternoon on the other side of the silk wall went by without Emmanuelle's having time to do anything but eat pastry, drink tea, and leaf through a magazine that the stewardess had given her (she refused to accept a second one because she did not want to be distracted from the novelty of flying).

Then a waiter placed a little table in front of her and served various foods that were hard to identify, in unusually shaped containers. Her dinner seemed to last for hours but the discovery of the culinary game pleased her so much that she was in no hurry for it to end.

She felt light and carefree. She noticed that she had even lost her dislike of the twins. The stewardess came and went, never failing to say something cheerful to her as she passed. When she was absent, Emmanuelle was no longer impatient.

She wondered if it was time to go to sleep. But actually she was free to sleep whenever she chose in that winged cradle so far from the surface of the earth, in a region of space where there were neither winds nor clouds, and where she was not sure there was even night and day.

* * *

Emmanuelle's knees were bare in the golden light shining down from overhead, and the man was staring at them. Under the invisible nylon, the movement of their dimples made agile shadows in the toasted-bread color of their skin. She knew the excitement they caused. They seemed more naked than ever under the spotlight which had been turned on them. She felt as if she were coming out of the water after a moonlight swim. Her temples throbbed faster and her lips filled with blood. She closed her eyes and saw herself not partially but totally naked, and she knew that once again she would be helpless against the temptation of that narcissistic contemplation.

She resisted, but only to increase the joy of gradually slipping into surrender. Its nearness was announced by a diffuse languor, a kind of warm consciousness of her whole body, a desire for abandon, for opening, for fullness; nothing very different from the physical satisfaction she would have felt from stretching out on the warm sand of a sun-drenched beach. Then, little by little, the surface of her lips became still more lustrous, her breasts swelled, and her legs tensed, attentive to the slightest contact. Her brain began experimenting with images. They were disconnected and formless at first, but were enough to moisten her mucous membranes and arch her back.

The steady, subdued, almost imperceptible vibrations of the metal fuselage attuned her body to the frequency. Starting from her knees, a wave rose along her thighs, resonating on the surface, moving higher and higher, making her quiver.

Phantasms assailed her—lips pressed against her skin, genitals of men and women (whose faces remained ambiguous), penises eagerly rubbing against her, pushing their way between her knees, forcing her legs apart, opening her sex, penetrating it with laborious efforts that enraptured her. One after another, they plunged into the unknown of her body, thrusting into her unendingly, sating her flesh, and endlessly emptying their semen into her.

Thinking Emmanuelle was asleep, the stewardess cautiously tilted back her seat, transforming it into a bed, and spread a cashmere blanket over her long, languid legs. The man stood up and pushed his seat back to the same level as hers. The children had already dozed off. The stewardess wished everyone a good night and turned off the ceiling lights. Only two purple night lights prevented objects and people from losing all shape.

Emmanuelle had abandoned herself to the stewardess's care without opening her eyes. Her reverie, however, had lost none of its intensity or urgency. Her right hand now began to move over her belly, very slowly, restraining itself, descending toward her pubis. The thin blanket undulated above it. Her fingertips, pushing down on the soft silk of her skirt, whose narrowness made it difficult for her to spread her legs, found the bud of flesh in erection that they sought and pressed it tenderly. Her middle finger began the gentle, careful motion that would bring on orgasm. Almost immediately, the man's hand came down on hers.

She stopped breathing and felt her muscles and nerves tighten, as though her belly had been struck by a jet of ice water. Her sensations and thoughts were suspended, like a film when the projector has stopped, leaving a single image on the screen. She was neither afraid nor offended. She waited for what was going to follow her collapsed dreams.

The man's hand did not move. Merely by its weight, it applied pressure to her clitoris, on which her own hand was resting.

Nothing else happened for some time. She then became aware that his other hand was lifting the blanket and drawing it aside. It took hold of her knee and felt its curves and hollows. It rose slowly along her thigh and soon passed over the top of her stocking.

When it touched her bare skin, she started for the first time and tried to break the spell. She sat up awkwardly and turned halfway on her side. As though they wanted to punish her for her futile revolt, the man's hands abandoned her abruptly. But before she had time to react, they were on her again, this time at her waist. They deftly unfastened and unzipped her skirt, pulled it down to her knees, then moved up again. One of them slipped under her panties and caressed her flat, muscular belly, just above the high mound of her pubis, stroking it as though it were the neck of a thoroughbred. Its fingers ran along the folds of her groin and across the top of her pubic hair, tracing a triangle whose area they seemed to be estimating. The lower angle was very wide, a rather rare feature that had been appreciated by Greek sculptors.

Then the hand forced her thighs to spread farther apart. It closed over her warm, swollen sex, caressing it as if to soothe it, without haste, following the furrow of its lips, dipping in lightly between them, passing over her erect clitoris and coming to rest on the thick curls of her pubis. As they moved to and fro between her legs, the fingers sank deeper between her moist membranes, slowing their advance, and seeming to hesitate as her tension increased. Biting her lips to stifle the sob that was rising from her throat, she panted with desire as the man brought her closer and closer to orgasm without letting her reach it.

Then his hand stopped moving and cupped the whole part of her body that it had inflamed. He leaned toward her, extended his other hand, took one of hers, and drew it inside his trousers. He helped her to grasp his rigid penis and guided her movements, regulating their length and cadence to suit his taste, slowing or accelerating them according to his degree of excitement, until he was convinced that he could rely on her intuition and good will and let her continue the manipulation in her own way.

She sat up to let her arm do its work properly, and he moved closer to her so that she could be sprayed by the sperm he felt welling up from the depths of his glands. He succeeded in restraining himself for a long time, while her bent fingers rose and fell, becoming less timid as they prolonged their caresses, no longer limiting themselves to elementary back-and-forth motions, but opening slightly, skillfully, to slide along the big, swollen vein of his arched penis (lightly scratching it with their filed nails), as far down as possible, as close to his testicles as the tightness of his trousers would permit, then rising again with lascivious twists. His member had grown so much that it seemed endless, but she finally reached its tip and covered it with the folds of loose skin in the hollow of her damp palm before beginning another downward journey, squeezing him tightly again, stretching his foreskin, alternately strangling his tumescent flesh and relaxing her grip on it, barely grazing it or tormenting it, massaging it in broad strokes or irritating it with quick, merciless little movements . . .

When his satisfied penis finally disgorged its semen in long, white, odorous spurts, she received it with strange exaltation along her arms, on her bare belly, on her throat, face, and mouth, and in her hair. It seemed that it would never stop. She felt as if it were flowing down her throat, as if she were drinking it . . . She was seized with an unknown intoxication, a shameless delight. When she let her arm fall, he took hold of her clitoris with his fingertips and brought her to orgasm.

A buzzing sound indicated that the loudspeaker was about to be used. The stewardess's voice, deliberately softened so the passengers would not be awakened too abruptly, announced that the plane would land at Bahrein in about twenty minutes.

It would leave at midnight, local time. A light meal would be served at the airport.

The light in the compartment gradually came on again, imitating the slowness of a sunrise. Emmanuelle used the blanket, which had slipped down to her feet, to wipe away the sperm that had spattered her. She pulled her skirt up over her hips. When the stewardess came in, Emmanuelle was sitting up on her seat, without having raised its back, still trying to make herself presentable.

"Did you sleep well?" the stewardess asked.

Emmanuelle fastened the waist of her skirt. "My blouse is all wrinkled," she said.

She looked at the damp spots that spread out in both directions from below her collar. She rolled back the lapels of her blouse and the pink tip of a breast appeared. Her neckline remained open and four pairs of English eyes were glued to the profile of her bare breast.

"Don't you have anything to change into?" asked the stewardess.

"No," said Emmanuelle.

The two women looked each other in the eye and recognized their complicity; they were both equally excited. The man observed them. There was not a single wrinkle in his suit, his shirt was as neat as when he had boarded the plane, his tie was perfectly straight.

"Come with me," said the stewardess.

Emmanuelle stood up, stepped past the man, and followed the young English stewardess into the ladies' lounge. It was filled with mirrors, cushioned footstools, white leather upholstery, and shelves laden with lotions in crystal bottles.

"Wait."

The stewardess slipped away and returned moments later, carrying a little suitcase. She lifted its calfskin lid and removed a russet sweater of orion, wool, and silk, so light that it was crumpled into a ball that fit into her closed fist. When she shook it out it seemed to swell suddenly like a balloon. Emmanuelle clapped her hands with admiration. "You're lending it to me?" she asked.

"No, I'm giving it to you. I'm sure it will look good on you."

"But . . ."

The stewardess put her finger over Emmanuelle's lips as they rounded to protest her embarrassment. Her tender eyes sparkled. Emmanuelle could not look away from them. She moved her face close to them. But the stewardess spun around and handed her a bottle of toilet water. "Rub yourself with this, it's delightful!"

Emmanuelle refreshed her face, arms, and neck, started to wipe between her breasts with the pad she had saturated with the perfumed liquid, then changed her mind and quickly unbuttoned the rest of her blouse.

She made it fall to the white carpet by throwing back her arms. Suddenly dizzied by her half-nakedness, she took a deep breath. She turned to the stewardess and looked at her with candid jubilation. The stewardess bent down, picked up the rumpled blouse, and pressed it against her face. "Oh, it smells so good!" she said, laughing mischievously.

Emmanuelle was disconcerted. The reminder of the incredible scene in her compartment seemed out of place to her now. Her only thought, which was turning in her mind as though in a cage, was to get rid of her skirt and stockings, to be completely naked for that beautiful girl. Her fingers were already toying with the buckle of her belt.

"How thick and black your hair is!" the stewardess exclaimed, playfully running a brush over the waves that hung down Emmanuelle's naked back to below her waist. "It's so shiny, so silky! I wish my hair were as beautiful as yours."

"But I like yours!" protested Emmanuelle.

Oh, if only the stewardess would undress, too! Emmanuelle desired her so much that her voice was husky when she implored: "Isn't it possible to take a bath on this plane?"

"Of course. But you'd better wait—the bathrooms at the airport are more comfortable. Anyway, you wouldn't have time, we're going to land in five minutes."

Emmanuelle was unable to resign herself. She pulled on the zipper of her skirt.

"Hurry and put on my sweet little sweater," the English girl said reproachfully, handing it to her.

She helped her put her head through the narrow opening. The elastic sweater was clinging and thin, the tips of her breasts stood out as visibly as if they had been painted reddish brown. The stewardess seemed to notice them for the first time. "What a seductive sight!" She pressed on one of the sharp nipples with her forefinger, as though she were ringing a doorbell. Emmanuelle's eyes twinkled.

"Is it true," Emmanuelle asked, "that all airline stewardesses are virgins?"

The English girl burst out laughing, then, before Emmanuelle had time to react, she opened the door and pulled her outside. "Go back to your seat, quickly! The red light is on, we're about to land."

Emmanuelle scowled. Aside from everything else, she had no desire to sit with the man in her compartment again.

The stopover was boring. What good did it do to know she was in the Arabian desert if she could see nothing of it? The airport building, aseptic and chromed, too glaringly lighted, refrigerated, airtight, and soundproof, bore a singular resemblance to the interior of the artificial satellite in the televised newscast that was being shown in the waiting room. She glumly took a bath, then drank tea and ate pastry with four or five other passengers, one of whom was "her" man.

She looked at him with astonishment, trying to understand what had taken place between them an hour earlier. That episode did not fit in with the rest of her life. But thinking about it was too complicated, too risky. She began making diligent efforts to empty the part of her brain that persisted in asking questions.

By the time the movement of the others, rather than the incomprehensible voice of the loudspeaker, told her she had to return to the plane, she was no longer quite sure of what it was that she was trying so hard to forget.

When the passengers were back aboard the plane, they saw that it had been cleaned, tidied up, and aired. Fresh perfume had been sprayed in the compartments. The reclining seats were covered with new blankets. Big, luminously white pillows, swollen with down, made the midnight-blue velvet on which they rested still more tempting. The steward came to ask if anyone would like a drink. No? Well, then, sleep well. The stewardess also came in to wish everyone a good night. That ceremony delighted Emmanuelle. She felt herself becoming happy again—in a positive way, wholeheartedly, with certainty. She wanted the world to be exactly as it was. Everything on earth was absolutely right.

She lay back in her seat. She lifted her legs one after the other, bending and unbending her knees, working the muscles of her thighs, rubbing her ankles together with a soft rustling of nylon.

"After all," she mused, "it's not just my knees that are worth looking at, but all of my legs. No one can deny that they're really pretty; they're like two little brooks covered with dry leaves and swollen with perversity, amusing themselves by passing over each other. And they're not the only good things about me. I also like my skin, and the way it turns golden in the sun, like a grain of corn, without ever reddening. I like my behind, too. And the tiny little raspberries at the tips of my breasts, with their collars of red sugar. I wish I could lick them . . ."

The ceiling lights dimmed. With a sigh of well-being, she pulled up the blanket, scented with a fragrance of pine needles.

When only the night lights were on, she turned over on her side and tried to see the man. Till now, when she had stretched out beside him, she had not dared to look at him directly. Her gaze met his. They looked into each other's eyes for a moment, with no expression other than one of perfect tranquillity. She recognized the spark of slightly amused and protective interest that she had noticed when they first met. (When had that been, exactly? Was it only seven hours ago?) The expression on his face was what she liked most about him.

His presence suddenly became agreeable to her again. She smiled and closed her eyes. She had a vague yearning for something, but did not know what. She found no other diversion than to resume rejoicing at being beautiful; her own image lingered in her head like a favorite refrain. Her heart beat faster as she sought in her mind the invisible cove that she knew to be buried under its promontory of black grass, where the two brooks came together, and she felt their current licking at its edges. When the man raised himself on one elbow and leaned toward her, she opened her eyes and let him kiss her. The taste of his lips on hers had the freshness of sea salt.

When he began pulling off her sweater she sat up and lifted her arms to make it easier for him. She relished the excitement of seeing her breasts emerge from under the russet garment, looking even rounder and larger in the near-darkness than in daylight. To leave him the whole pleasure of undressing her, she did not help him when he groped for the zipper of her skirt, although she did raise her hips so that he could slide it down without difficulty. This time her narrow skirt did not remain twisted around her knees—she was completely free of it.

His active hands rid her of her thin panties. When he had unhooked her garter belt, she rolled down her stockings herself and dropped them to the floor in front of her seat, where they joined her skirt and sweater.

Only when she was entirely undressed did he take her in his arms and begin caressing her from her hair to her ankles, forgetting nothing. She now had so powerful a desire to make love that her heart hurt and her throat was constricted. She thought she would never be able to breathe again, to return to daylight. She was afraid, she felt like calling out, but the man was holding her too tightly, putting one hand between her buttocks, widening the quivering little crevice, with one whole finger buried in it. At the same time he kissed her avidly, licking her tongue, and drinking her saliva.

She whimpered softly without knowing the exact cause of her distress. Was it the finger that was probing so deeply inside her, or the mouth that was feeding on her, swallowing each breath, each gasp? Was she tormented by desire or ashamed of her lasciviousness? She was haunted by the memory of the long, arched form that she had held in her hand, magnificent and erect, arrogant, hard, unbearably hot. She moaned so loudly that the man took pity on her. She at last felt his bare penis, as big as she had expected, touch her belly, and she pressed against it with all the softness of her body.

They remained like that for a long time, without moving; then, seeming to make up his mind abruptly, he lifted her in his arms, drew her over him, and put her down beside him in his seat, on the aisle.

She was less than three feet away from the English children. She had forgotten they even existed; she now realized that they were not asleep and that they were looking at her. The boy was nearer to her, but the girl had huddled against him to see better. Motionless and breathless, they were staring at her with widened eyes in which she could see nothing but fascinated curiosity. At the thought of being possessed in front of them, of abandoning herself to that excess of debauchery, she felt a kind of dizziness. But at the same time she was eager to begin and let them see everything.

She was lying on her right side with her legs bent forward while the man held her by the hips from behind. He slipped one leg between hers and entered her with a straight, irresistible thrust that was made easy by the absolute rigidity of his penis and the moistness of her flesh. It was not until he had reached the deepest point of her vagina and stopped there long enough to sigh with pleasure that he began moving his member back and forth with long, regular strokes.

Delivered of her anxiety, she panted, became warmer and more liquid with each onslaught of his phallus. Through the mist of her ecstasy, she marveled at the thought that her organs had not atrophied during all the months when they had not been stimulated by a male goad. Now that she was rediscovering that pleasure, she wanted to enjoy it as long and completely as possible.

The man showed no sign of being about to tire. For a moment she wondered how long he had been in her, but there was no way for her to guess the time that had gone by.

She held back her orgasm, effortlessly and without frustration, because she had trained herself since childhood to prolong the pleasure of waiting. Even more than the final spasm itself, she loved that growing sensitivity, that extreme tension of her being, which she knew so well how to give herself when she was alone, and her fingers stroked the trembling stem of her clitoris for hours, with the lightness of a violin bow, refusing to yield to the supplication of her own flesh, until at last the pressure of her sensuality broke through. The explosion was as terrifying as the convulsions of death, but she was always reborn from it immediately, fresher, and more alert than ever.

She looked at the children. Their faces had lost their haughtiness; they had become more human. They were neither excited nor snickering, but attentive and almost respectful. She tried to imagine what was going on in their heads, the bewilderment they must be feeling at the event they were witnessing, but her thoughts unraveled, her brain was seized with spells of faintness, and she was much too happy to care about anyone else.

When the acceleration of her partner's movements, a certain stiffness of his hands as they gripped her buttocks, and the sudden expansion and pulsation of the organ that was piercing her made her realize that he was about to ejaculate, she let herself go. The spurting sperm whipped her pleasure to a frenzied pitch. During the whole time he was emptying himself in her he stayed deep in her vagina, pressed against her cervix, and even in the midst of her spasm she still had imagination enough to enjoy the mental image of his penis disgorging creamy torrents that were lapped up by the oval opening of her uterus, as greedy and active as a mouth.

He finished his orgasm and she too became calm, filled with a sense of well-being without remorse, increased by his sliding motion as he withdrew, the contact of the blanket that she felt him spreading over her, the comfort of the reclining seat, and the warm, increasing opacity of the sleep that was covering her.

The plane had passed through the night as though crossing a bridge, blind to the deserts of India, to the bays, estuaries, and rice paddies below. When Emmanuelle opened her eyes, the mountains of Burma were iridescent in the light of a sunrise that she could not see, while inside the compartment the purple glow of the night lights left her unaware of the exotic landscape and the time of day.

The white blanket had slid off her lap and she was lying naked, curled up like a cold child. Her conqueror was asleep.

Awakening by degrees, she lay still. Nothing of what she might have been thinking could be seen on her face. She slowly stretched her legs, drew back her shoulders, and rolled over on her back, groping for the blanket. But her hand stopped in midair—a man was standing in the aisle, looking at her.

From his position above her, he seemed gigantic and she told herself that he was also incredibly handsome. That was no doubt why she forgot her nakedness, or at least was not embarrassed by it. "He's a Greek statue," she thought. A fragment of a poem, which was not Greek, flashed into her mind: "Deity of the ruined temple . . ." She wished there were primroses and yellowed herbs strewn at the feet of the god, and foliage twined around his pedestal. Her gaze moved from the short, soft hair that curled above his ears and forehead down the straight bridge of his nose, to his delicately curved lips, and his marble chin. Two firm tendons sculpted the lines of his neck down to where they met his shirt, half-open over a hairless chest. Her eyes continued to study him. There was an enormous bulge beneath his white flannel trousers, near her face.

The apparition bent down, picked up her clothes scattered over the floor—skirt, sweater, panties, garter belt, stockings, and shoes—then straightened up and said, "Come."

She put her feet down on the carpet and took the hand he was holding out to her. Then, having stood up with a lithe effort, she walked forward, naked, as though altitude and the night had brought her into a different world.

The stranger led her into the lounge where she had already gone with the stewardess. He leaned his back against the silk-padded wall and placed her so that she was facing him. She nearly cried out when she saw the reptile that had risen before her from its patch of golden underbrush. Because she was much shorter than he was, the blunted triangle of his glans touched her between her breasts.

He took her by the waist and lifted her effortlessly. She clasped her fingers over the back of his neck and felt his muscles harden beneath her palms, then, when he lowered her onto his penis, she spread her legs so that it could penetrate her. Tears flowed down her cheeks while he entered her cautiously, tearing her. Pressing her knees against his hips and the wall, she did her best to help the herculean serpent crawl into the depths of her body. She writhed, clawed his neck as she clung to it, sobbed, moaned, and cried out unintelligible words. In her frenzy she was not even aware that he was ejaculating, quickly, with such a savage thrust of his pelvis that he seemed determined to force his way through her till he reached her heart. When he withdrew, with his face radiant, he kept her standing against him. His wet phallus cooled her smarting skin. "Did you like it?" he asked.

Emmanuelle put her cheek on the Greek god's chest. She felt his semen moving in her. "I love you," she murmured. "Do you want to take me again?"

He smiled. "I'll come back," he said, "Get dressed now." He bent down and kissed her on the hair so chastely that she did not dare to say anything more. Before she had realized that he was leaving her, she found herself alone.

With slow gestures, as though she were performing a rite (or because she had not yet entirely recovered the rhythm of reality), she turned on the shower and let the water flow over her, covered her body with lather, carefully rinsed herself, rubbed her skin with warm, fragrant towels, sprayed her neck, armpits, and pubic hair with a perfume that evoked the greenery of a forest, and brushed her hair. Her image was reflected on three sides by long mirrors. It seemed to her that she had never been so fresh or aglow with more beauty. Would the stranger return as he had promised?

She waited till the loudspeaker announced that the plane was approaching Bangkok. Then, resentfully, with her heart in turmoil, she dressed and returned to her compartment. She took her bag and her jacket from the baggage rack and put them on her lap when she sat down. An obliging hand had raised the back of her seat and placed a cup of tea and a tray of rolls beside it. The man in the next seat, whom she glanced at absent-mindedly, was visibly surprised. "But . . . aren't you going on to Tokyo?" he asked in English, with a note of dismay in his voice.

Emmanuelle guessed rather easily what he had said and shook her head. His face darkened. He asked another question, which she did not understand and, anyway, was in no mood to answer. She looked straight ahead with a chagrined expression.

He took out a notebook and held it in front of her, motioning her to write in it. He probably wanted her to leave him her name, or an address where he could reach her. But she shook her head again, stubbornly. She wondered if the stranger with the smell of warm stone, the fantastic genie of the ruined temple, would get off at Bangkok with her or fly on to Japan.

She looked for him among the passengers when they had gotten off the plane and were waiting, clustered under its wings in the morning of the tropical airport, for someone to lead them to the cement and glass buildings whose futuristic silhouettes stood out against a sky that was already white with heat. But she saw no one as tall as he or who had his autumnal hair. The stewardess smiled at her; Emmanuelle scarcely noticed her. She was already being pushed toward the iron customs gates. Someone crossed a barrier, flashed a pass, and called her. She ran forward with a cry of joy and threw herself into the outstretched arms of her husband.

2
Green Paradise

Do I counsel you to kill your senses?
I counsel the innocence of the senses.

—Friedrich Nietzsche,
Thus Spake Zarathustra

The black mosaic pool with pink water in which Emmanuelle's ankles were dancing belonged to the Royal Bangkok Sports Club. The wives and daughters admitted into that male club came to the paddock of the racecourse on Saturday and Sunday afternoons to show their legs and breasts through the transparency of their dresses. On the other days of the week, they did not leave the edges of the swimming pool.

Lying next to Emmanuelle, who occasionally felt the caress of her short hair on her thigh, a young woman was talking with the side of her face resting on her folded arms. The swelling of her muscles beneath her bronzed skin outlined her coltish body in the sunlight like the red chalk of a sculptor's rough sketch. Her happy laughter echoed from the surface of the water. The beauty of her voice adorned the stories she was telling.

"Gilbert thinks it's good form to pretend to be outraged since *The Buccaneer* passed through. He's still complaining about the three nights I spent away from home, but God knows I came back like a good little girl on the fourth night—once *The Buccaneer* was gone!"

Emmanuelle knew that this was Ariane, wife of Count de Saynes, Counselor to the French Embassy, and that she was twenty-six.

"What's the matter with your husband?" asked another woman who was stretched out on a red deck chair, combing the fur of a blasé little female dog that she called "O." "Is he abandoning his principles?"

"It wasn't the nights I spent in the captain's cabin that upset him, but the fact that I didn't tell him about it before-hand. He feels he made himself ridiculous by looking for me everywhere and even notifying the police."

The hum of conversation continued. Spread out on the hot flagstones in a half-dazed stupor despite being used to the broiling climate, the women formed a star around Ariane, lying on her stomach, and Emmanuelle, sitting on the edge of the pool. Emmanuelle heard them more than she saw them; for the moment, the sight of their browned bodies interested her less than the caramel-colored glints of the warm water around her legs.

"Where did he expect you to be? He doesn't have to be a genius to figure it out."

"Just when you finally had a chance to enjoy yourself a little in this place!"

"Especially since he saw me for the last time at the end of the party on board the ship, in the clutches of two lusty seamen who seemed determined to share me as their booty."

"Did they do it?"

"How should I know?"

Ariane lifted her bust to speak to Emmanuelle, who could not help admiring the ease and guile with which these ceramic sunbathers untied the tops of their swimsuits, ostensibly to avoid leaving a light streak in their tan, actually to make the law of gravity work in their favor when, with apparent innocence, they raised themselves on their elbows to greet a passing male friend.

"My dear," Ariane proclaimed, "you missed the chance of the century. Last weekend an adorable little warship anchored in the river to pay some sort of courtesy visit to the Thai Navy. I wish you could have seen it! A crew of satyrs, with a Dionysian captain! For three days there were nothing but cocktail parties, dinners, dances—and all the rest!"

Emmanuelle was intimidated by the indiscretion, the shrill laughter, and the free-and-easy manner of the young women around her; she was surprised that her experience as a Parisian was of so little help to her in confronting this intemperate society. The idleness and luxury of these uprooted French girls seemed to her more excessive than the languid luxuriance of the wealthy women of Auteuil and Passy. Emmanuelle's new acquaintances even lived their idleness intensely, ostentatiously, without improvisation or respite. And apparently, wherever they were, whatever their age, looks, or condition, their sole concern, day in and day out, was to seduce or be seduced.

One of them, with a tawny mane that tumbled profusely over her shoulders and down to her hips, casually got up, walked to the edge of the pool, and stood there, stretching and yawning with her legs wide apart. The crotch of her white bikini, no wider than a shoelace, revealed a tuft of sun-drenched pubic hair the color of a lion cub's fur and the curve of her sex, a strong, well-exercised sex whose immodesty was heightened by the purity of her face and the grace of her figure.

"Jean is no fool," she said, "he waited till *The Buccaneer* was gone before he sent for Emmanuelle."

"It's a pity," Ariane remarked in a tone of sincere regret. "She would have been a tremendous success."

"But I don't see why he should have thought Emmanuelle was safer in Paris," one of the half-naked girls said ironically. "I'm sure she wasn't neglected there!"

Ariane looked at Emmanuelle with what seemed to be increased interest.

"That's true," one of her acolytes commented phlegmatically. "Her husband must not be jealous if he left her alone like that for a whole year."

"It wasn't a year, it was only six months!" Emmanuelle corrected her. She scrutinized the rounded contours of the vulva which was so close to her that she could have touched it with her lips by leaning forward slightly.

"I think he was right not to bring you with him when he came here," said O's mistress. "He was in the north most of the time during the last few months; he didn't even have a house and he had to stay in a hotel whenever he was in Bangkok. It wouldn't have been a decent life for you." And she added immediately, "How do you like your villa? I hear it's delightful."

"Oh, it's not really finished yet; it still lacks some furniture. What I like most about it is the garden, with its big trees. You'll have to come and see it," Emmanuelle concluded politely.

"You'll still be alone in Bangkok for three-quarters of the year, won't you?" asked a member of Ariane's retinue.

"Of course not," Emmanuelle replied with a touch of irritation. "Now that the engineers are all settled in Yarn Hee, Jean won't have to go there any more. He'll have plenty to do at the main office. He'll stay with me all the time."

"It doesn't matter," Ariane said with a reassuring laugh, "Bangkok is a big city."

Since Emmanuelle did not seem to understand why the size of the city was important, Ariane explained: "The office will take up most of his time, you'll see. You'll have all the time and space you need for maneuvering your admirers. It's lucky all the able-bodied men in this country aren't as busy as our husbands! Do you drive?"

"Yes, but I'm afraid of getting lost in that tangle of impossible streets. Jean is giving me the chauffeur until I've learned to find my way around."

"It won't take you long to learn what you need to know. And I'll guide you."

"In other words, Ariane will see to it that you're led astray!"

"Nonsense! Emmanuelle doesn't need me for that. But I *would* like her to tell me about her escapades. Minoute is right—Paris is the only place where you can really swing."

"I have nothing to tell," Emmanuelle objected weakly. She felt almost wretched.

"Don't worry," said the one who seemed most eager to know her secrets, "we'll be as quiet as the grave."

"But what can I tell you? During the whole time I was in France," Emmanuelle said with sudden strength and serenity, "I never deceived my husband."

Silence reigned among the women for a few moments. They seemed to be evaluating the scope of that declaration. Emmanuelle's tone of sincerity had impressed them. Ariane looked at her with a little disgust. Was this girl a prude? And yet, judging from her bathing suit . . .

"How long have you been married?" she asked.

"Nearly a year," answered Emmanuelle. And she added, to make them jealous of her youth, "I was married at eighteen." Then she said abruptly, for fear of letting them regain the advantage, "A year of marriage, and half of it away from each other! You can imagine how glad I am to be with Jean again." The young women nodded, as though to show that they understood her feelings. Actually they were thinking, "She's not one of us."

"Would you like to come to my house for a milk shake?"

Until now, Emmanuelle had not noticed the girl who had just leaped to her feet. But she was already amused by the expression of firmness and almost protective self-assurance of this new face—because it was also the face of a little girl.

Not so little, she corrected herself, as the adolescent standing before her seemed to take charge of her. Around thirteen, probably, but almost as tall as Emmanuelle. The difference was in the maturity of their bodies; there was still something unfinished, something undeveloped, about the girl's. But it was perhaps the texture of her skin that made her closest to childhood. The sun had given it no patina, it was not a warm-colored, civilized, elegant skin like Ariane's. Emmanuelle even judged it, at first sight, to be a little rough . . . But not really. It was as though she had a very slight case of goose flesh. On her arms, especially. It was glossier on her legs. Beautiful boyish legs, because of the prominent tendons in their ankles, their hard knees and calves, their sinewy thighs. It was their harmonious proportions and their light strength that made them pleasant to look at, rather than the somewhat impure emotion generally aroused by women's legs. Emmanuelle could more easily imagine them running over a beach or flexing on a diving board than loosened by the caress of a hand and opening the door of a docile body to an impatient one.

She got the same impression from the girl's concave, athletic belly, hollowed by her vivacity, palpitating like a heart, with all the tonicity of its aligned muscles. The narrowness of the cloth triangle that partially covered it—no more than what a nude dancer wears on the stage—did not succeed in making it indecent. Her pointed little breasts were scarcely concealed by the symbolic ribbon of her bikini top. "They're pretty," thought Emmanuelle, "but why doesn't she just leave them bare? They would look even better and I'm sure they wouldn't give anyone any lewd thoughts." After a moment's consideration, she was no longer so sure. She wondered what sensuality such young breasts could have. Then she remembered her own and the pleasures she had drawn from them while they were still so small that they made almost no difference in her profile; they had not even been as big as the girl's, she acknowledged, for as she looked at the girl's closely they seemed more prominent. Maybe it had been the contrast with Ariane's breasts that had influenced her judgment at first. Or the girl's narrow hips, or her childish waist . . .

Or perhaps also the long, thick braids that played over her pink chest. Emmanuelle had never seen such hair. So blonde, so fine that it was almost colorless—neither straw, nor flax, nor sand, nor gold, nor platinum, nor silver, nor ash . . . To what could it be compared? To certain skeins of raw silk, not completely white, used for embroidering. Or to the sky at dawn. Or to the fur of the lynx . . . Then Emmanuelle encountered the girl's green eyes and forgot everything else.

Slanting, oblong, rising toward her temples with such a rare line that they seemed to have been placed in that light Caucasian face by mistake. But so green, it was true! So luminous! Emmanuelle saw flashes pass through them like the revolving beam of a lighthouse, flashes of irony, seriousness, reason, extraordinary authority, then sudden solicitude and even compassion, followed by laughing mischievousness, whimsy, or candor—spellbinding flashes.

"My name is Marie-Anne."

And no doubt because Emmanuelle, absorbed in contemplating her, had forgotten to answer, she repeated her invitation: "Would you like to come to my house?"

This time Emmanuelle smiled at her and stood up. She explained that she could not accept today because Jean was to pick her up at the club and take her visiting. She would not be back until rather late. But she would be so happy if Marie-Anne would come to see her the next day. Did she know where she lived?

"Yes," Marie-Anne said briefly. "All right, tomorrow afternoon."

Emmanuelle took advantage of the diversion to escape from the group, saying that she did not want to keep her husband waiting. She hurried toward her cabana.

"Do you think the guest room could be ready in a few days?" Emmanuelle's husband asked her when they sat down to dinner.

The folding walls, pushed back now, opened onto a rectangle of water in which lotuses, pink, purple, white, or blue in the morning, nodded their green calyxes in the evening.

"It can be used right now, if necessary. Only the curtains and multicolored cushions I want to put on the bed are missing. Ah, yes, a lamp, too."

"I'd like it to be completed a week from Sunday."

"I'm sure it will be. It won't take ten days to put in those things. But what do you want to do with it? Is someone coming?"

"Yes, Christopher . . . you know, he's been in charge of the Malaysian office for the past month. I invited him before you came. He's just answered. It's worked out perfectly . . . the company is sending him on a tour of Thailand, so he'll be able to spend several weeks with us. He's a very nice fellow, you'll see. It's been almost three years since I saw him last."

"Isn't he the one who stayed with you at Aswan after the dam was built?"

"Yes, he was the only one who didn't lose his nerve."

"I remember now. You told me how serious he was . . ."

Jean laughed at her pout. "He's serious, yes, but he's not gloomy. I like him, and I'm sure you will, too."

"How old is he?"

"He's six or seven years younger than I am. He was just out of Oxford at the time."

"He's English?"

"No. Only half . . . his mother is English. But his father is one of the founders of the company. Don't think he's a spoiled brat, though. He's a hard worker. You can rely on him."

Emmanuelle was a little disappointed to learn that her intimacy with Jean would be disturbed so soon after she had regained it. Even so, she decided to give a warm welcome to the visitor who meant so much to him. She recalled having seen photographs showing Christopher as a tanned, athletic explorer with a reassuring smile, and, after all, she would rather have him as a guest than the paunchy old inspectors whom she would later, no doubt, have to guide through the sights of the city, protecting them from sunstroke and mosquitoes.

She asked about other details, avid for images of the dangerous years before Jean had met her. If he had been killed then, she would never have become his wife. This thought made her heart tighten and she was unable to continue eating.

The houseboy moved around the table, bringing coconuts filled with custard and caramel, after the polished rice and the flower fritters that the old cook with red teeth had spent three days preparing in honor of the new mistress. He walked by rising alternately on the ball of each foot, as if he were about to leap. Emmanuelle was a bit afraid of him. He made too little noise, he was too strong and lithe, too neat, too ubiquitous— too much like a cat.

Marie-Anne arrived in a white American car driven by an Indian chauffeur with a turban and a black beard. He left as soon as she had gotten out. "Will you be able to drive me home, Emmanuelle?" she asked.

Emmanuelle was struck by her familiarity and also noticed, more than the day before, how much Marie-Anne's voice was in harmony with her braids and her skin. She had an impulse to kiss the girl on both cheeks, but something held her back. Was it the pointed little breasts under her blue blouse? Ridiculous!

Marie-Anne was standing close to her. "Don't pay any attention to the stories those idiots tell," she said. "They're always bragging. They don't do a tenth of what they say they do."

"Of course," Emmanuelle agreed after taking a second to realize that Marie-Anne was referring to the older women at the pool. "Shall we sit on the terrace?"

Marie-Anne accepted the proposal with a nod. They went up to the second floor. As they were passing the door of her bedroom, Emmanuelle suddenly remembered the big nude photograph of her that Jean kept by his bed, and she was afraid her guest would see it. She quickened her pace, but

Marie-Anne had already stopped in front of the mosquito netting that separated the bedroom from the landing.

"Is that your bedroom?" she asked. "May I see it?"

She went inside without waiting for an answer. Emmanuelle followed her. Marie-Anne burst out laughing. "What an enormous bed! How many people sleep in it with you?"

Emmanuelle blushed. "It's actually two twin beds pushed together."

Marie-Anne looked at the photograph. "You're beautiful. Who took it?"

Emmanuelle wanted to lie by saying that Jean had taken it, but she was unable to do so. "An artist, a friend of my husband," she admitted.

"Do you have any other pictures? He must not have taken only this one. Don't you have any that show you making love?"

Emmanuelle felt slightly dazed. What kind of a little girl was this who looked at her with those big green eyes and that bright smile, and asked such astounding questions in a tone of camaraderie, with no apparent emotion? And the worst of it was that, perhaps because of those eyes, Emmanuelle felt that she could do nothing but tell the truth, and that this child had the power to make her confess all her secrets if she wanted to. She abruptly opened the door, as though that act could protect her. "Shall we go?"

Marie-Anne smiled fleetingly. They went out onto a terrace that was sheltered from the sun by a yellow and white striped awning. A warm breeze was blowing from the nearby river.

"You're so lucky!" Marie-Anne exclaimed. "There's no other house in Bangkok with a location like this. What a wonderful view, and what a comfortable feeling!"

Marie-Anne stood still for a moment before the landscape of coconut palms and flame trees. Then, with a natural movement, she unfastened her high raffia belt and tossed it onto one of the wicker chairs. Without further delay, she unzipped her colorful skirt, let it drop to the floor, and stepped out of the circle it formed around her feet. Her blouse came down to her hips, below the sides of her panties, so that nothing could be seen of them, front and back, but a narrow, crimson, lace-trimmed vertical strip. She sprawled on one of the deck chairs and picked up a magazine, not wasting a minute.

"It's been so long since I saw any French magazines! Where did you get these?" She stretched out at ease, with her legs sedately joined.

Emmanuelle sighed, drove away the confused thoughts that were assailing her, and lay down facing Marie-Anne, who burst out laughing.

"What kind of a story is this, 'Owl Oil'? Do you mind if I read it now?"

"Of course not, Marie-Anne."

She plunged into the story. The open magazine hid her face. She did not remain motionless long. Her body became animated with sudden starts, like the shying of a colt. She raised her knee, and her left thigh, no longer pressed against her right one, leaned gently on the arm of the chair.

Emmanuelle tried to look into the gap of her panties. One of Marie-Anne's hands left the magazine, moved between her open legs, pushed aside the nylon, sought a point farther down, found it, and stayed there for a moment. Then it rose again, uncovering, as it passed, the groove in her flesh. It played over the swelling beneath the cloth, descended, slipped under her buttocks, and began the same itinerary again. But this time only her middle finger was lowered; the others, gracefully raised, flanked it like the open wings of an insect. It brushed against her skin until her wrist, abruptly bent, came to rest. Emmanuelle felt her heart beating so hard that she was afraid it could be heard. Her tongue was thrust forward between her lips.

Marie-Anne continued her game. The middle finger pressed down more deeply, pushing her flesh aside. It stopped again, drew a circle, hesitated, patted, and vibrated with an almost invisible movement. An uncontrolled sound came from Emmanuelle's throat. Marie-Anne lowered her magazine and smiled at her.

"Don't you caress yourself?" she asked in surprise. She leaned her head on her shoulder with a sly look. "I always caress myself when I read."

Emmanuelle nodded her approval, incapable of speaking. Marie-Anne dropped her magazine, arched her back, put her hands to her hips, quickly pushed her red panties down over her thighs, and kicked her legs in the air until the panties were off. Then she relaxed, closed her eyes, and separated her pink mucous membranes with two fingers. "It feels good there," she said. "Don't you think so?"

Emmanuelle nodded again.

"I like to take a long time," Marie-Anne went on in a tone of ordinary conversation. "That's why I don't touch the top too much. It's better to go back and forth in the crack." Her actions illustrated her precept.

She finally raised the small of her back and moaned faintly. "Oh! I can't hold myself back any more!"

Her finger fluttered on her clitoris like a dragonfly. Her moan became a cry. Her thighs opened violently and snapped shut on her hand, imprisoning it. She cried out for a long time, in an almost heart-rending way, and fell back, panting. A few seconds later, when she had caught her breath, she opened her eyes. "It's really too good," she mused.

Inclining her head again, she put her middle finger into her sex, cautiously, delicately. Emmanuelle bit her lips. When Marie-Anne's finger had entirely disappeared, she heaved a long sigh. She was radiant with health, a clear conscience, and the satisfaction of having fulfilled a duty. "Caress yourself, too," she said encouragingly.

Emmanuelle hesitated, as though looking for a way out. But her confusion did not last long. She suddenly stood up, opened her shorts, and took them off. She was wearing nothing under them. Her orange sweater accentuated the gloss of her black pubic hair.

When Emmanuelle lay down again, Marie-Anne came and sat at her feet, on a soft plush-covered ottoman. They were now both dressed alike—chest covered, naked from the waist down. Marie-Anne looked at Emmanuelle's sex from close up.

"How do you like to caress yourself?"

"Why, the same as everyone else!" said Emmanuelle, unsettled by the light breath on her thighs.

Marie-Anne could have released her from the tension of her senses, and also from her embarrassment, by putting her hand on her. But she did not touch her. She merely said, "Show me."

At least masturbation gave Emmanuelle immediate relief. It seemed to her that a curtain was being hung between her and the world, and, as her fingers accomplished their familiar mission between her legs, peace descended upon her. This time she did not try to prolong the pleasure of waiting. She needed to find a base, a known terrain, quickly; and she knew none better than the dazzling refuge of orgasm.

"How did you learn to come, Emmanuelle?" Marie-Anne asked her when she calmed down.

"I taught myself—my hands discovered it all by themselves," Emmanuelle replied, laughing. She felt cheerful now, and in a mood for talking.

"Did you already know how to do it when you were thirteen?" Marie-Anne asked dubiously.

"Of course. I'd known for a long time by then. And you?"

Marie-Anne refrained from answering and pursued her inquiry. "What's your favorite place to caress yourself?"

"Oh, I have several. The sensation is different at the tip, or on the side, or at the bottom. And the tiny little opening just below—you know, the urethra—is also very sensitive. All I have to do is touch it with my fingertips and I come immediately. Isn't it the same with you?"

Marie-Anne again ignored the question. "What else do you do?"

"I like to caress myself inside my labia, where it's wettest."

"With your fingers?"

"Yes, and also with bananas." Emmanuelle's voice took on a ring of pride. "I push them all the way in. I peel them first. They mustn't be ripe. The long green ones that you can buy here at the floating market . . . I can't tell you how good they are!" She was so captivated by the images of her solitary delights that she had almost forgotten Marie-Anne's presence. Her fingers kneaded her vulva. She wished something would penetrate it now. It was absolutely necessary for her to have another orgasm. She rubbed her joined fingers against the insides of her labia with large, regular, rapid movements for several minutes, until she was relieved.

"You see, I can caress myself several times in a row."

"Do you do it often?"

"Yes."

"How many times a day?"

"It depends. In Paris I was away from home most of the time—at the university, or shopping. I could never make myself come more than once or twice in the morning, when I woke up, or while I was taking my bath. Then two or three times before I went to sleep, and whenever I happened to wake up during the night. But when I'm on vacation I have nothing else to do, so I can caress myself much more. And my life here is going to be one long vacation!"

They were both silent for a time, close to each other, savoring the friendship that was being born of their frankness. Emmanuelle was happy that she had been able to overcome her timidity and speak of those things. And she was especially happy, though she did not dare admit it to herself, that she had masturbated in front of a girl who liked to watch and knew how to come. In her heart, she was already adorning Marie-Anne with all sorts of merits. And she looked so pretty now! Those elfin eyes . . . And that thoughtful groove that formed a pout on her lower face, as expressive, distant, and full-lipped as the pout on her upper one! And those thighs, open without embarrassment, heedless of their nudity . . .

"What are you thinking about, Marie-Anne?" she asked. "You look so serious!" And she playfully pulled one of her braids.

"I'm thinking about bananas," said Marie-Anne. She wrinkled her nose and they both laughed till they were breathless.

"It's good not to be a virgin any more," remarked Emmanuelle. "Before, no bananas! I didn't know what I was missing."

"How did you begin with men?"

"It was Jean who deflowered me."

"You hadn't had anyone before that?" exclaimed Marie-Anne.

She was so obviously scandalized that Emmanuelle answered apologetically, "No. Well, not really. Boys used to caress me, of course, but they didn't know how to go about it very well!" She recovered her self-assurance. "Jean made love with me from the start. That's why I loved him!"

"From the start?"

"Yes, the day after I met him. The first day, he came to our house—he was a friend of my parents. He kept looking at me with an amused expression. He managed to be alone with me and asked me questions about everything—how many boyfriends I had, whether I liked to make love. I was terribly embarrassed, but I couldn't help telling him the truth. It was almost the same as with you! And he wanted all kinds of details, too. The next afternoon he invited me to go for a ride in his beautiful car. He told me to sit close to him and he immediately caressed my shoulders, then my breasts, while he was driving. Finally he stopped on a little road in the Fontainebleau forest and kissed me for the first time. He said to me, in a way that completely reassured me about what was going to happen, 'You're a virgin and I'm going to take you.' And we sat for a long time without talking or moving, pressed against each other. Finally my heart stopped pounding so much. I was happy. It was happening exactly as I might have dreamed it would, although actually I'd never dreamed about it. Jean told me to take off my panties myself and I quickly did so, because I wanted to cooperate in my defloration, not submit to it passively. He made me lie on the seat of the car. The top was down and I could see the green heads of the trees. He stood in the opening of the door. He didn't begin by caressing me. He entered me immediately, but in such a way that I don't remember feeling any pain. Far from it! I came so much that I fainted or fell asleep, I don't know which. In any case, I don't remember a thing until the restaurant in the forest where we had dinner. It was wonderful! Afterward, Jean asked for a room and we went on making love until midnight. It didn't take me long to learn!"

"What did your parents say?"

"Nothing. The next day I went around proclaiming that I was no longer a virgin and that I was in love. They seemed to think it was perfectly normal."

"And Jean asked you to marry him?"

"Certainly not! Neither of us had any idea of getting married. I was only seventeen, and barely out of school. And I was too glad to have a lover, to be a man's 'mistress.'"

"Then why did you get married?"

"One day Jean announced to me calmly, as always, that his company was sending him to Thailand. 'I'm going to marry you before I leave,' he said without further ado. 'You'll join me later, when I have a house for you to live in.'"

"How did you feel about it?"

"I laughed wildly. A month later, we were married. My parents had considered it only natural for me to be Jean's mistress, but they protested violently when he talked about marrying me. They tried to convince him that he was too old, that I was too young, even 'too innocent'! What do you think of that? But it was Jean who convinced them. I wish I knew what he said to them. My father must have been hard to persuade. He couldn't resign himself to seeing me drop my math."

"What math?"

"I'd begun studying mathematics at the university."

"What ever gave you such an idea?" asked Marie-Anne, laughing.

"Well, I love math. Jean was supposed to leave a short time after our wedding, but luckily he was delayed for six months, so we weren't separated right away. I was able to be his wife as long as I'd been his mistress. And I found that it was as much fun to be married as it was to be a sinner, although at first it seemed odd to make love at night."

"What happened afterward? Where did you live while he was gone? With your parents?"

"Of course not! I lived in his apartment, or rather *our* apartment."

"He wasn't afraid to leave you all alone like that?"

"Afraid? Of what?"

"That you'd deceive him, naturally!"

Emmanuelle laughed. "I don't think so. We never talked about it. It must not have occurred to him. It didn't to me, either."

"But you still did it, didn't you?"

"No. Why? Lots of men ran after me. They seemed ridiculous to me . . ."

"Then what you told the girls wasn't a lot of nonsense?"

"The girls?"

"Yesterday, have you forgotten already? You told them you'd never gone to bed with any man but your husband."

Emmanuelle hesitated for a fraction of a second. That was long enough to put Marie-Anne on the alert. She pivoted, knelt, and leaned over the arm of the chair, radiating suspicion.

"There's not one word of truth in all that," she said accusingly. "I can tell from your face. You ought to see how frank you look!"

Emmanuelle tried to be evasive, without conviction. "First of all, I never said any such thing . . ."

"What? You didn't tell Ariane that you hadn't deceived your husband? That's exactly why I wanted to talk to you. Because I didn't believe you. Luckily!"

Emmanuelle maintained her sophistry. "Well, you're wrong. And I repeat that I didn't say what you claim I did. I merely said that I'd been faithful to Jean the whole time I was in Paris. That's all."

"What do you mean, that's all?"

Emmanuelle forced herself to appear nonchalant while Marie-Anne examined her face. Then Marie-Anne abruptly changed her tactics. Her voice became caressing.

"Anyway, why on earth should you have been faithful to him? There was no reason for you to deprive yourself."

"I didn't deprive myself. There was no one I wanted. It's quite simple."

Marie-Anne pursed her lips, reflected, then asked, "Are you saying that if there *had* been someone you wanted, you'd have made love with him?"

"Certainly."

"How can you prove it?" Marie-Anne challenged, in the acid tone of a quarrelsome child.

Emmanuelle looked at her undecidedly, then said all at once, "I did it."

Marie-Anne seemed electrified. She jumped up, sat down again, cross-legged, and put her hands on her knees.

"You see?" she said in an outraged and hurt tone of voice. "And you tried to make me think you didn't!"

"I didn't do it *in Paris*," Emmanuelle explained patiently. "I did it *on the plane*. The plane that brought me here. Now do you understand?"

"With whom?" Marie-Anne asked skeptically.

Emmanuelle took her time before answering. "With two men. I don't know their names."

If she had thought she was going to cause a sensation, she was disappointed. Marie-Anne resumed her interrogation without showing any reaction. "Did they come in you?"

"Yes."

"Were they very deep inside you?"

"Oh, yes!" Emmanuelle instinctively put her hand to her belly.

"Caress yourself while you tell me about it," Marie-Anne ordered. But Emmanuelle shook her head. She seemed to have been suddenly tongue-tied. Marie-Anne examined her critically. "Go on," she said, "talk!"

Emmanuelle obeyed. She was reluctant and embarrassed at first, but soon, excited by her own story, she gave all the details without having to be questioned. She stopped after telling how the Greek statue had ravished her. Marie-Anne had been listening with a studious expression, changing her posture several times, but she did not seem to be particularly impressed.

"Have you told Jean?" she asked.

No."

"Have you seen those two men again?"

"Of course not!"

It seemed that, for the moment, Marie-Anne had nothing more to ask.

Emmanuelle called the little servant girl—straight out of one of Gauguin's dreams, with her flowery black hair, her ocher body, and her scarlet sarong—and asked her to make some tea. She put on her shorts again. Marie-Anne put on her panties, but left her skirt on the floor. She then demanded to see all of Emmanuelle's pictures of herself naked. When Emmanuelle had brought them to her, she recovered her caustic attitude.

"Listen, you're not going to tell me you didn't do anything with the photographer, are you?"

"He didn't even touch me!" Emmanuelle protested. "And," she added, with pretended rancor, "besides, I didn't have a chance—he was a fag."

Marie-Anne turned down the corners of her lips. She was still skeptical. She studied the pictures again. "I think an artist should always go to bed with his model before making a portrait of her. It was silly of you to choose someone who didn't like women."

"I didn't choose him," said Emmanuelle, beginning to feel genuinely irritated. "It was his idea. As I've already told you, he was a friend of Jean's."

Marie-Anne made a gesture that seemed to sweep away that past. "You really ought to have yourself painted by a good artist. It'll be too late when you're old."

The image of what Marie-Anne must have meant by a "good artist," and the idea of the imminence of her own old age, sent Emmanuelle into a fit of laughter. "I don't like to pose, not even for a photograph, so for a painting . . ."

"And haven't you done anything with men since you've been here?"

"Don't be ridiculous!" Emmanuelle said indignantly.

Marie-Anne seemed preoccupied and almost disheartened. "One of these days you'll have to find yourself a lover," she sighed.

"Is it really necessary?" asked Emmanuelle.

But Marie-Anne was apparently in no mood for joking. She shrugged with annoyance. "You're odd, Emmanuelle," she said. Then, after a silence, "You don't intend to go on living like an old maid, do you?" And she repeated, seized with a kind of anger, "You're odd, really!"

"But I'm not an old maid," Emmanuelle pleaded timidly, "I have a husband!"

This time Marie-Anne merely answered with a cold look. She seemed to find Emmanuelle's argument pitiful, and to have no interest in continuing the discussion. But now it was Emmanuelle who did not want to change the subject. She tried to re-create the mood. "Don't you want to take off your panties?"

Marie-Anne shook her braids. "No, I have to leave." She stood up. "Are you going to take me home?"

"Why are you in such a hurry?" Emmanuelle complained. But she had already realized that Marie-Anne's decisions were irrevocable.

In the car, Marie-Anne gave her a look of serious concern and said, "You know, I don't want you to waste your life, you're too pretty. It's stupid for you to be as prudish as you are."

Emmanuelle laughed loudly. But Marie-Anne did not give her time to make an ironic reply. "It's incredible that you've gotten this old without ever having had anything but those worthless little adventures in your windowless airplane." She shook her head sadly. "You're not normal, take my word for it."

"Marie-Anne . . ."

"Never mind . . . But there's no use moaning over the past." Her green eyes glowed. "From now on, will you at least do what I tell you?"

"What do you want me to do?"

"Everything I tell you."

"Well . . ." said Emmanuelle, fascinated.

"Will you give me your word?"

"Oh, all right, if it amuses you." She continued smiling, but Marie-Anne did not let herself be diverted from her solemnity.

"Shall I give you some advice?"

"No, thanks!"

The elfin eyes analyzed the seriousness of her case. She tried to maintain a casual attitude, without deluding herself about her chances of holding her own against Marie-Anne.

When the car stopped in front of the bank that her father managed, Marie-Anne said, "At exactly midnight tonight, caress yourself again. I'll be doing the same thing at the same time."

Emmanuelle blinked her eyes as a sign of complicity. She leaned out the window to throw a kiss to Marie-Anne, who called back to her, "Don't forget!"

Only after she was gone did Emmanuelle realize that she had not been able to ask her a single question. She had told that little girl with braided hair everything about her private life, but she knew nothing about hers. She had even forgotten to ask if she was a virgin.

That night, when Jean had taken his shower and come into the bedroom, he found Emmanuelle kneeling on the edge of the big, low bed, naked. She put her arms around his hips and took his penis in her mouth. She had sucked it no more than a few seconds when it swelled and stood up. She passed it back and forth between her lips until it was very hard, then she licked it all over, tilting her head, pressing the blue vein that lay just under the skin, making it grow larger and more congested beneath her kiss. Jean told her that she looked as if she were eating an ear of corn and she bit him lightly with her little teeth to complete the analogy. She quickly redeemed herself by drawing the satiny skin of his testicles into her mouth. She lifted them in her hands, slipped the end of her tongue under them, caressed another vein, gorged herself on the warm blood she felt pulsing more strongly at the touch of her lips, explored more and more intimately, searched, moved forward and back, abruptly returned to the end of his penis, pushed it to the bottom of her throat, so deeply that she nearly choked, and there, without withdrawing it, she slowly and irresistibly pumped it while her tongue enveloped and massaged it.

Her hands clung to the small of his back with a passion that increased as she sucked him more regularly and the excitement of her lips and her tongue was communicated to her breasts and her sex. Between her joined thighs she felt a liquid flowing like the saliva that was now bathing his apoplectic member in her warm mouth. So that she could moan with pleasure and let a partial orgasm relieve her and enable her to continue her fellatio, she took her lips away from his penis for a moment, though without ceasing to caress its opening by licking it tenderly with the tip of her tongue. Then she again swallowed the bridge of palpitating flesh that bound them together.

Jean took her head between his hands, but it was not because he wanted to guide her movements or regulate their rhythm. He knew he would be better off if he left everything to her and let her refine their common pleasure as she saw fit. As always, the style she adopted this time would be different from any she had ever used before. Sometimes she played at keeping him in suspense. She would settle down somewhere, flit from one sensitive spot to another, ignore the moans and pleas she drew from her victim's throat, make him twitch and pant, and drive him into a frenzy until at last she put the deft, precise finishing touch to her work. But this time she chose to dispense a more serene satisfaction. Without holding his vibrant penis too tightly, she added the pressure of her fingers and the regular movement of her hand to the suction of her lips, intent on delivering his organ of its semen and emptying it as totally as possible. When he surrendered, she sipped the substance she had succeeded in drawing from deep inside him; but, purring, she let the last spurt melt on her amorous tongue.

She herself was so close to orgasm that he was able to bring it on by simply pressing her clitoris between his lips.

"In a little while, I'll take you," he said.

"No, no! I want to drink you again! Promise! Promise you'll come back to my mouth. Oh, I want you to flow into my mouth again! Say you'll do it, please! It's so good! I like it so much!"

"When I wasn't here, did your other women caress you as well as I do?" she asked him later, when they were both resting.

"How could they? There's no one who can compare to you."

"Not even Thai women?"

"No."

"Aren't you just saying that to please me?"

"You know I'm not. If you weren't the best of mistresses, I'd admit it to you—to help you improve. But I really don't see what more you could learn. After all, there must be a limit to the art of love."

Emmanuelle seemed thoughtful. "I don't know." She frowned. The sound of her voice showed that her doubt was unfeigned. "In any case, I'm sure I'm still a long way from the limit."

"What makes you think that?" exclaimed Jean.

She did not answer.

"You don't think I'm a good judge?" he insisted.

"Oh, yes!"

"Not a good teacher, then? You seem to be suddenly dissatisfied with your amorous education."

She hastened to reassure him. "Darling! No one in the world could have taught me better than you. But it's hard to explain . . . I have a feeling that in love there must be something more important, more intelligent than simply knowing how to make it well."

"Are you referring to devotion, congeniality, tenderness?"

"No, no! I'm sure the something important I'm talking about is related to physical love. But that doesn't mean it's a matter of more knowledge, skill, or ardor. It may be a state of mind, a mentality." She caught her breath. "I don't know, actually, if it's a question of a limit, either. Suppose it were a question of a viewpoint, a way of seeing things . . ."

"A different way of looking at love?"

"Not only love. Everything!"

"Can't you explain yourself more clearly?"

She woefully thrust out her lips and rolled the curls of her pubic hair around her long, pearly fingernails, as though to help herself meditate.

"No," she concluded, "it's not clear in my mind. I know there's some kind of progress I have to make, something I lack and have to find before I can be a real woman, really your wife. But I don't know what it is!" Her voice became sorrowful. "I thought I knew so many things, but what are they, compared to what I don't know?" She frowned with impatience. "The first thing I have to do is to become more intelligent. You see, I don't know anything, I'm too innocent. I'm too virginal. It's horrible how virginal I feel tonight! Virginal all over, bristling with virginity. It's shameful."

"My pure angel!"

"Oh, no, not pure! Not pure at all! A virgin isn't necessarily pure. But she's necessarily stupid."

He kissed her, delighted with her. She persisted: "A virgin is full of prejudices."

"It's adorable to hear you complaining about your innocence when I've just been ravished by your chaste lips!"

Her face brightened, but was she convinced? "Ah, if that's really how a girl gets her intelligence, I won't let another minute go by without learning more from you."

This reminder had an effect on him that she did not take long to discover. Ready to carry out her promise, she sat up and put her tongue out between her wet teeth . . . But he held her back. "Who told you that intelligence entered only through *that* mouth. It's like the wind—it blows where it pleases."

He lay on her and she immediately wanted to be taken as much as he wanted to take her. She opened her sex herself, with her fingertips. She guided his glans and helped it to plunge into her. Her knees rose, flanking his body, while his hardened organ sank into her belly as it had sunk into her throat a short time earlier. She wished she could feel it in her mouth at the same time. The exuberance of her imagination made up for what was lacking in reality—her lips, licked by her tongue, believed they could taste the salty sweetness of his sperm. She dreamed she was drinking it; the pleasure of her belly filled her throat and she said imploringly, "Come in me!"

She felt that the orifice of her womb, at the bottom of her vagina, had fused with his phallus and was sucking it inward. She wanted him to ejaculate; she tried, with all the persuasion of her belly and hips, to draw his vital fluid from him. Each muscle of her body did its part to make her a supple, agile animal, clinging to him and making him tremble with pleasure. But he wanted to overcome her, to make her reach orgasm first. He stabbed her rapidly and violently with the full length and thickness of his penis, not sparing her, clenching his teeth; he avidly listened to her moans, smelled her fragrance, felt her warmth and watched her while she writhed and winced as though beneath a whip, clawed his neck and finally cried out so loudly and so long that she became breathless and suddenly calm, dazed, humbled, serene, scarcely feeling her body, but already eager for the excitement to be reborn in her mind.

She wanted him to lie still for a moment. He knew it and remained motionless, his cheek against hers. The tide of her night-black hair caressed his lips. They stayed that way for they did not know how long. Then he heard her gasping in his ear: "Am I dead?"

"No. I'm your life." He embraced her and she quivered. "Oh, my love, it's true that we're one. I'm only a piece of you." She put her lips to his and kissed him with all the strength and tenderness of her mouth. "Take me again! Deeper! Open me. Tear me . . . Come in my heart!" She begged him and, at the same time, laughed at her own absurdity. "Deflower me! Oh, I love you! Deflower me!"

He took up the game. "Give yourself more. Yield. Be compliant. Do whatever I want."

"Yes!" she murmured, intoxicated with submission. "Yes! Do anything you want. Don't ask me. Do it!"

She wished she could surrender still more, be more obedient, more obliging, more open. "Is there any greater happiness than consenting?" she elatedly asked herself. This thought was enough to drive her across the thin line that separated her from orgasm.

Then, when she was again a felled animal, a happy trophy in the shadow of the hunter, she said, "Do you think I'm the woman you want?"

He contented himself with kissing her.

"But I want to become that woman even more!"

"You do, every day."

"Are you sure?"

He smiled at her confidently. She stopped worrying. A nocturnal current was flowing in her veins, making her sluggish, closing her lips. She tried to fight the pleasure that was blurring her mind.

"It must have been Marie-Anne who got me upset like that," she heard herself saying, to her own surprise, because that was not what she wanted to confide to Jean.

"Why Marie-Anne?"

"She's a very sophisticated little girl."

Emmanuelle no longer felt like talking, but Jean insisted.

"Do you think she's the one who's going to reveal the mysteries of life to you?"

"Why not?"

The idea amused him. "Have you already had a glimpse of her talents?"

She hesitated a little and finally said "No," so absorbed in another world that she did not care whether he believed her or not. Then she smiled at an image that was not out of place on the shore where her dreams had landed. "But I'd like to!"

"I see," Jean said indulgently. He rocked her gently. "My little virgin wants to make love with Marie-Anne, doesn't she? Is that what's bothering you?"

She nodded methodically with the exaggeration that one puts into one's gestures when one wants to make oneself understood without opening one's eyes. "It's not only that, but it's surely that, too," she agreed.

He made fun of her benignly: "With a little girl!"

But a big spoiled-child pout already delineated her night face, and her voice protested from far away, deadened and withdrawn, as though from the trough of a wave: "I have a right to want to, haven't I?"

They lay side by side, joined at the shoulders and hips. She was careful not to move, so that not one drop would escape from her.

"Sleep," said Jean.

"Wait . . ."

From a distant room came the regular notes of a set of chimes. Her hand slowly descended to her belly. Her fingers touched her clitoris and penetrated her sex, gorged with sperm. She saw Marie-Anne's thighs open before her closed eyes, and to each caress in her dream she responded with an identical one. When she knew that Marie-Anne was about to surrender, she cried out even more loudly than she had done in Jean's arms. Propped up on one elbow, he smiled as he watched her reach her climax, naked and luminous with pleasure, with one hand held captive by her belly while the other alternately pressed both her breasts. Her legs quivered fitfully long after her forehead, eyelids, and lips had taken on the immobile softness of sleep.

3

Of Breasts, Goddesses, and Roses

In the midst of my own arms I made myself another woman.
—Paul Valéry, *La Jeune Parque*

Here, and till evening. The rose of shadows will turn on the walls. The rose of hours will silently shed its petals. The bright flagstones will lead as they please these steps in love with day.
—Yves Bonnefoy, *Hier régnant désert*

Emmanuelle wanted to go to the club to swim, not to listen to gossip, so she decided to go there in the morning. She swam the length of the pool ten times, lithely, caring nothing about the looks of the few men who were present at that hour. The repeated motion of her arms above her head had made her breasts come out of her strapless bathing suit. Each time she rolled on her side, the streaming water made their shape stand out and gave a satiny gloss to their skin. A fine circular furrow had appeared around their tips; the edges of their areolas thus seemed to be raised, forming an atoll. If it had not been for this detail, which recalled the vulnerability of their soft flesh and evoked its juicy taste, their contours might have been too perfect to be exciting; they might have looked too much like the breasts of a statue.

When, panting from this exercise, she took hold of the chrome uprights of the ladder, she saw that the exit was blocked. Ariane de Saynes was standing on the glazed edge of the pool, leaning over her.

"Roadblock!" she said, laughing. "Show your credentials!"

Emmanuelle was annoyed that one of the "idiots" had found her, but she smiled as best she could.

"So here you are, playing like a water sprite when honest women are doing their shopping! Why all this secrecy?"

"But you're here, too," Emmanuelle pointed out.

She tried to climb out of the pool. Ariane was in no hurry to let her pass.

"Ah, with me it's not the same thing," she said, with a show of mystery. But Emmanuelle did not ask her to elucidate.

Ariane calmly examined her prisoner's charms. "You're built divinely!" she said with admiration.

She pronounced her judgment in a tone of conviction and Emmanuelle told herself that, actually, she did not seem malicious. She might be a little wild, but there could be no doubt that she was stimulating, invigorating. Emmanuelle no longer had to force herself so much in order to be friendly.

Ariane finally stepped away from the ladder. Emmanuelle climbed out of the pool. She calmly pushed her breasts back into her bathing suit, or rather the lower half of her breasts (nearly all of the nipples remained visible), and sat down beside Ariane. Two tall, Nordic-looking young men came up and began talking to them in English. Ariane answered good-humoredly. It mattered little to Emmanuelle that she could not understand what they were saying. Ariane turned to her abruptly and asked, "Do these two appeal to you?"

Emmanuelle made a little grimace and Ariane notified the two candidates that they had failed. Apparently without rancor, they laughed loudly. But they still showed no inclination to leave. Emmanuelle thought they looked incredibly simple-minded. A short time later, Ariane stood up with determination and pulled her by the arm.

"They're boring. Come to the diving board with me."

The two women climbed up the twenty-five feet to the platform and lay on their stomachs, side by side, on the rope matting that covered it. Ariane quickly took off her two-piece bathing suit.

"You can sunbathe in the nude," she said. "From here, you can see people coming."

But Emmanuelle had no desire to be naked in front of Ariane at that moment. She stammered an unconvincing explanation —her tight bathing suit was not easy to take off and put on again . . . the sun was too hot . . .

"You're right," conceded Ariane. "It's better to get used to it gradually."

They soon sank into a semi-lethargy. Emmanuelle decided that, after all, Ariane had her good points. She liked people with whom she could be with without talking. It was Emmanuelle, however, who broke the silence.

"What can one do here, aside from the pool, cocktail parties, and social evenings here and there? Don't you finally get a little bored?"

Ariane whistled, as though she had just heard something outrageous.

"What an idea! There's no shortage of pastimes here! I won't say anything about movies, nightclubs, and other trifles like that. But you can ride, play golf, tennis, or squash, go water-skiing on the river, or drift along the canals in romantic melancholy. And you can visit pagodas too. Why not? There are close to a thousand of them. At the rate of one a day, you'll have enough to keep you busy for three years. Going to the sea is worth the trip. The beaches are fantastic, endlessly long and wide, lined with coconut trees, deserted, with seashells all over them. The water is fabulously phosphorescent at night, full of billions of little creatures. The coral tickles your feet. And the sharks come and eat out of your hand."

"I'd like to see that!" said Emmanuelle, laughing.

"They'll even sing you serenades, if you make love in their territory. During the day, in the sunlight, with the sand massaging you, or in the shade of the sugar palms. You can always find a little boy who's willing to fan you for a baht while your valiant knight is paying homage to you. And at night, lying on the beach at the edge of the surf, with your back caressed by the tongues of the waves and your eyes protected from the stars by an amorous face—ah, you really appreciate how lucky you are to be a woman!"

"If I understand you right," said Emmanuelle, without being scandalized, "that's the favorite sport in this country."

Ariane stared at her with an enigmatic smile and did not answer her immediately. "Tell me, my dear . . ." She stopped short, seemingly working out some mysterious probability.

Emmanuelle turned to her and laughed. "What would you like me to tell you?"

Ariane reflected in silence, then she abruptly decided how much confidence the newcomer deserved. Her voice lost the tone of urbane banter that it had kept till now. She gave Emmanuelle a friendly grin.

"I'm sure," she said, "that you have a passionate nature. You're not as prim and proper as you pretend to be. And I'm glad you're not. To tell you the truth, you interested me right away."

Emmanuelle did not quite know what to make of this declaration. Almost in spite of herself, she remained on the defensive. She was more put out than flattered, because she did not like anyone to question her frankness. And what made those girls keep thinking she was a prude? It had made her laugh at first, but now it was beginning to annoy her.

"Don't you want to enjoy yourself here?" Ariane went on in a tone that said more than her words.

"Yes," said Emmanuelle. She realized that she was venturing onto a dangerous path, but she was even more afraid of being suspected of virtue.

Ariane's smile of approval rewarded her only partially. "Then come with me some night, my pet. You can tell your husband you're having dinner with a group of women. You'll see what kind of a sewing circle I'll take you to! You could search forever and a day without finding bolder or more gallant warriors than mine. They're witty, young, and robust, and they know how to wield their weapons. You have nothing to fear. Will you come?"

"But you hardly know me," Emmanuelle said evasively. "Don't you . . ."

Ariane shrugged. "I know you well enough! I don't need to keep you under prolonged observation to know that you're beautiful enough to stun both men and women. And those I have in mind are experts when it comes to beauty. It would never occur to me to introduce you to them if I weren't sure of them and of you. So, you see?"

"And . . ." Emmanuelle hesitated. "What about your husband?"

Ariane's laugh was full of frankness. "A good husband likes his wife to be happy."

"I don't know if that will seem so normal to Jean."

"Then don't take him into your confidence," Ariane said jovially. She suddenly moved closer to Emmanuelle, put her arms around her waist, and hugged her. "Will you swear to tell the truth?"

Emmanuelle blinked without committing herself too much. The solid, warm breasts against her shoulder unsettled her a little, whether she cared to admit it or not.

"You won't go on trying to make me believe that your husband is the only man you've ever welcomed into that exciting body of yours, will you? Of course not. Well, have you told him about it every time?"

Emmanuelle felt tormented. The quest for confessions was beginning again! But what would be the use of defending herself? And why should she try to seem more innocent than she was? She shook her head in answer to Ariane's question.

Ariane kissed her gaily on the ear.

"You see!" she said triumphantly, contemplating her with pride. "I promise that you won't be sorry you came to Bangkok!"

Her tone seemed to imply that Emmanuelle had agreed to sign a pact. She tried to escape. "No, listen, I'm embarrassed . . ." All at once she became bolder. "Don't think it's out of prudishness, or for moral reasons. It's not that. But . . . at least give me time to get used to the idea . . . by degrees."

"Of course," said Ariane. "There's no rush. It's the same as with the sun." She seemed to have had a sudden inspiration; she let her lips sketch a furtive smile and sat up. "Come, we're going to have a massage."

She put on her bikini. Then, a little disdainfully, as though she were speaking to a small child, she added, "Don't be afraid, sweetie, only women will be there."

Emmanuelle left her car at the club and went with Ariane in her open convertible. They drove for half an hour through tricycle rickshaws and motorcycle taxis that spewed smoke into the streets lined with Chinese signs. They stopped in front of a new one-story building flanked by silk shops, restaurants, and travel agencies. The façade was adorned with an inscription in characters that were unknown to Emmanuelle. They opened a thick glass door and stepped into the reception room of a bathing establishment, little different in appearance from what it would have been in Europe. A Japanese woman in a flowered kimono greeted them politely, bowed to them several times with her hands crossed over her chest, before leading them along halls that smelled of steam and *eau de cologne*. She stopped in front of a door and bowed deeply again. Emmanuelle wondered if she was mute.

"You can go in here," said Ariane, "the masseuses are all good. I'll take the next cabin. We'll meet in an hour."

Emmanuelle had not expected Ariane to leave her. She felt a little disconcerted. The door that the Japanese woman had opened led into a small, clean, low-ceilinged room where a slender Thai girl in a white nurse's smock was standing between a bathtub and a massage table. She had the face of a bird that had returned from many journeys. She bowed also, then said a few words without seeming to care whether they were understood or not, came over to Emmanuelle, and began carefully unbuttoning her blouse.

When Emmanuelle was undressed, the masseuse motioned her to get into the bathtub, filled with bluish, fragrant, warm water. She passed a damp cloth over her face, then methodically lathered her shoulders, back, chest, and belly. Emmanuelle shivered as the sponge swollen with lather moved between her legs.

When she had finished bathing and drying her with a big, warm towel, the Thai girl motioned her to lie down on the padded table. First she hammered her lightly and rapidly with the edge of her hand, then pinched her muscles, pressed down on her thighs and back, pulled her toes, massaged the back of her neck for a long time, and patted her on the head. Half-dazed, Emmanuelle felt relaxed and happy in spite of everything.

The masseuse opened a cupboard, took out two devices the size of a cigarette pack, and attached them to the backs of her hands. They immediately began to make a humming sound. Her vibrating palms slowly crawled over Emmanuelle's naked body, sinking into everything that offered a cavity or a fold, slipping into the hollow of her neck, under her armpits, between her breasts, between her buttocks, with irresistible proficiency. Then they sought the most receptive spots on the inner surface of her thighs. Emmanuelle's flesh trembled. Her legs parted and she raised her pubis slightly, offering herself with an inimitably graceful movement that held out the lips of her sex as though for a childish kiss. But the hands moved away and rose toward her bust, coming and going with professional skill, making long, repeated sweeps like an iron smoothing a piece of percale. When Emmanuelle began moaning almost inaudibly, they climbed to her nipples and made circular motions on them, sometimes barely grazing them, sometimes pushing them down into the thickness of her breasts. Waves traveled through her all the way to the base of her spine. She arched her back and cried out plaintively for long minutes. The hands continued their work on her sensitive nipples until her orgasm died down, leaving her limp and inert.

Without wasting any time, the masseuse shifted to her shoulders, arms, and ankles. Emmanuelle was slowly returning to normal. She finally opened her eyes and smiled faintly. The masseuse smiled back at her stiffly and said something that sounded like a question. At the same time she moved her slender fingers toward Emmanuelle's belly, looking at her with her eyebrows raised, as though waiting for permission. Emmanuelle nodded. The hand, weighted by the vibrator, carefully made practiced movements on the surface of her sex and in its folds, knowing exactly what to do at each moment in order to give the greatest pleasure. Sure of the outcome, adding the virtuosity of its quivering, rubbing, and scratching to the power of the electric vibrations, it made no effort to be gentle, and gave Emmanuelle no respite.

She held back with all her strength, but her resistance was short-lived. She had another orgasm, so violent that even the masseuse's face showed a certain alarm. For a long time after the hands had been withdrawn from her, Emmanuelle continued writhing, gasping, clutching the edges of the white table with her fingers.

"The walls are supposed to be soundproof," Ariane said as they were leaving together, "but I heard you right through them. Now I hope you won't ever try to tell me you prefer mathematics."

Marie-Anne came to Emmanuelle's house on four afternoons in a row. She interrogated her more closely each time, demanding—and getting—new details about her relations with Jean and the incontinence of Emmanuelle's daily reveries.

"If you'd actually given yourself to all the men you've imagined doing it with," Marie-Anne observed one day, "you'd be an accomplished woman."

"You mean I'd be dead," retorted Emmanuelle, laughing.

"Why?"

"Do you think a woman can make love with men as often as she can make herself come by her own efforts?"

"Why not?"

"Listen, it's tiring to be taken by a man!"

"And caressing yourself never tires you?"

"No."

"How often do you do it now?"

Emmanuelle smiled modestly. "I did it a lot yesterday. At least fifteen times, I think."

"There are some women who do it that often with men."

Emmanuelle nodded. "Yes, I know," she said, though she did not seem tempted. "Men aren't always so exciting, you know. They're heavy, they're hard, sometimes they even hurt you. And they don't necessarily know the way a girl likes to come best . . ."

Paradoxically, there was only one subject about which she could not bring herself to speak frankly. She barely alluded to it now and then, awkwardly, unable to discern whether Marie-Anne understood or not. She herself had difficulty in understanding a shyness and discretion that nothing in her visitor's conduct seemed to justify. Marie-Anne always undressed as soon as she arrived. She had readily discarded her blouse the first time Emmanuelle had suggested it to her, and from then on they spent their time together naked, on the terrace surrounded by foliage. But Emmanuelle showed her excitement only by caressing herself more often. She did not dare to touch Marie-Anne or invite her to touch her, even though she wanted it so much that it kept her awake at night. A strange modesty and a strange immodesty were battling for her soul. She sometimes wondered—though confusedly and without allowing herself to think about it too deeply—whether that unwonted reserve was not actually a new and superior refinement invented without her knowledge by the intuition of her senses, and whether the deprivation of Marie-Anne's body that she thus inflicted on herself, against all instinct and reason, did not ultimately have a more subtle savor, a more perverse attraction, than physical intimacy might have had. And so instead of suffering, as she normally would have, from that situation in which a little girl manipulated her at will without granting anything to her desire in return, she discovered in it an unexpected source of sensual delight.

Just as an unknown pleasure had thus arisen from the frustration of what had always seemed to her the most natural of all carnal desires, and the one she prized most highly, another erotic value had been revealed to her by the remarkable secrecy that Marie-Anne maintained with regard to her own sex life. When she noted the ease with which she resigned herself to knowing nothing, or almost nothing, about Marie-Anne, Emmanuelle realized that she had more cerebral and physical enjoyment from giving another girl a lewd spectacle than she would have gotten from witnessing it herself. She eagerly looked forward to Marie-Anne's arrival every day, but it was now less for the excitement of seeing her naked or watching her lascivious games than for the infinitely more scandalous, and therefore more delectable, excitement of caressing herself, stretched out on her deck chair, before her friend's attentive gaze. When Marie-Anne was gone, the spell was not broken— Emmanuelle would imagine her green eyes fixed on her sex and continue masturbating until evening.

On the Wednesday following their first meeting, Emmanuelle was invited to tea by Marie-Anne's mother. In the pretentiously furnished drawing room she found a dozen "ladies" who all seemed equally insignificant. Marie-Anne was sitting demurely on the rug, absorbed in her duties as a model little girl. Emmanuelle was already regretting that they could not be alone when her interest was revived by the arrival of a very elegant young woman who, at first sight, appeared to be as much out of place as herself.

Emmanuelle was reminded of the Parisian models she had loved. The young woman had the same tall, slender figure, the same imponderable lassitude and illusory remoteness. Her mouth, partly open "like a rose," her amber eyebrows raised above immense eyes, and the winsome curve of her eyelashes gave her face a look of ingenuousness so improbable that it seemed an act of bravado. Emmanuelle told herself intolerantly that she was the only one present who, because of what she called her "experience," could discern the modesty in that totally studied elegance, the captivation in all that passion hidden beneath the detachment of a lustrous gaze. She recalled having thus discovered in her friends' faces, "borrowed from the proudest monuments," what Baudelaire had meant in condemning "movement that displaces lines." The alabaster goddesses had been made flesh, but Man, who believed only in inaccessible paradises and inanimate gods, had kept his desire for statues, and the worshiped flesh had become stone again.

This evocation was now charged, for Emmanuelle, with an ambiguous emotion in which the still-recent savor of her schoolgirl ardors was mingled with the more adult frenzies that she had known in fitting rooms.

Before her mother had time to introduce the newcomer, Marie-Anne stood up and drew Emmanuelle into a corner of the drawing room where they could not be overheard. "I have a man for you," she said with the satisfied look of having accomplished a mission.

Emmanuelle could not help laughing. "Now there's a real piece of news! And what a way you have of announcing it! What do you mean by 'a man for me'?"

"He's Italian and very handsome. I've known him a long time but I wasn't sure he was the man you needed. I thought it over and decided he was. You have to meet him without wasting any time."

This note of urgency, typical of Marie-Anne, amused Emmanuelle once again. She was not at all certain that the candidate, whoever he might be, was "the man she needed," but she did not want to disappoint her mentor. So she did her best to show interest in her plan, although she felt little gratitude for her concern.

"What's he like, this handsome man of yours?" she asked.

"He's a perfect Florentine marquis. I'm sure you've never met anyone so distinguished. He's slender and tall, with an aquiline nose, black, deep, piercing eyes, a dark complexion, a bony face . . ."

"Ah!"

"What? Don't believe me if you don't want to. But I'm sure you won't have that foolish smile on your face when you see him. He was born under the sign of Leo, too."

"Who else is?"

"Ariane and I."

"I see. Then . . ."

"But he has black, shiny hair like yours. With just enough silver in it to make it look elegant."

"Gray hair! He must be an old man!"

"Naturally. He's the right age for you, exactly twice your own—thirty-eight. That's why I'm telling you to hurry; next year you'll be too old. Furthermore, he won't be here next year."

"What's he doing in Bangkok?"

"Nothing. He's very intelligent. He roams through the country, he knows everything. He goes to excavate ruins, he studies the ages of Buddhas. He's even found things in the museum that the man in charge had never seen there. I think he wrote a book about it. But, as I said, mostly he does nothing."

"Tell me," Emmanuelle interrupted brusquely, "who's that fantastic girl?"

'What fantastic girl?"

"The one who just came in."

"Came in where?"

"*Here,* Marie-Anne! Are you getting stupid? Over there, look, straight in front of you . . ."

"Are you talking about Bee?"

"What did you say?"

"I said 'Bee'! You're the one whose mind is slipping."

"Bee? What an odd name!"

"Oh, it's not a name. It's the English word for *abeille* if it's spelled *b* double *e*."

"But how does *she* spell it?"

"The way I tell her to."

"Come, come, Marie-Anne!"

"It's not her real name, of course. I'm the one who gave it to her. By now everyone has forgotten the other one."

"Tell it to me anyway."

"What difference would it make? You wouldn't be able to repeat it. It's an outlandish English name, completely unpronounceable."

"Even so, you don't expect me to call her Bee, do you?"

"You don't need to call her anything."

Emmanuelle looked at Marie-Anne with surprise, hesitated, then contented herself with asking, "She's English?"

"No, American. But don't worry, she speaks French as well as you and I. She doesn't even have an accent; it would be quainter if she did."

"You don't seem too fond of her."

"Bee? She's my best friend!"

"Are you serious? Why haven't you told me about her?"

"I can't tell you about all the girls I know."

"But if you like her so much, you could have at least mentioned her to me."

"What makes you think I like her that much? She's my friend, that's all. That doesn't necessarily mean I like her."

"Marie-Anne! How do you expect anyone to make sense of what you're saying? The truth is that you don't want to tell me about anything that concerns you. And you don't want me to know your friends. Are you jealous? Are you afraid I'll take them away from you?"

"I don't see what good it would do to waste your time with a bunch of girls."

"Don't be silly! My time isn't all that precious. You sound as if you thought my days were numbered."

"Well . . ."

Marie-Anne seemed to believe it so seriously that Emmanuelle was upset. "I don't feel decrepit yet," she protested.

"Oh, it comes on very fast, you know."

"And that Bee, does she also have one foot in the grave, according to your calculations?"

"She's twenty-two years and eight months old."

"I see! Is she married?"

"No, not even married."

"Then she's even more of an old maid than I am. I can imagine how you must talk to her!" Marie-Anne made no comment. "You don't intend to introduce me to her, do you?" Emmanuelle asked.

"All you have to do is come with me! Instead of standing there spouting nonsense."

Marie-Anne made a signal to Bee, who came forward to meet them. "This is Emmanuelle," said Marie-Anne, as though she were revealing the perpetrator of a crime.

Seen from close up, Bee's big gray eyes gave an impression of intelligence and freedom. She was apparently as little inclined to dominate others as she was to let herself be easily ruled. Emmanuelle told herself that Marie-Anne surely had her hands full with this girl. She felt avenged.

They exchanged innocuous banalities. Bee's voice went well with her eyes. Its delivery was steady, without hesitation, and it was warmed by an intimate gaiety. Emmanuelle thought that she had the face and the tone of voice of happiness.

She asked how Bee spent her days. Mainly strolling around the city, it seemed. Did she live alone in Bangkok? No, she had come a year ago to visit her brother, who was a naval attaché at the American Embassy. She had at first intended to stay only a month, but, as it turned out, she was still there. She was in no hurry to leave.

"When I've had enough of this prolonged vacation," she said, "I'll get married and go back to America. I don't want to work. I love having nothing to do."

"Are you engaged?" asked Emmanuelle.

This question let her discover Bee's laugh. It was forthright and very pretty.

"In my country, you get engaged the day before your wedding; and two days before, you don't yet know who you're going to marry. Since I don't intend to retire tomorrow or the day after, I have no idea who my husband will be."

"But getting married doesn't necessarily mean retiring," protested Emmanuelle.

Bee smiled indulgently. She merely said "Oh," with an intonation of doubt; then she added, "There's nothing wrong with retiring."

Emmanuelle almost asked, "Retiring from what?" But she was afraid of being indiscreet. It was Bee who asked her, "Are you glad you married so young?"

"Oh, yes! It's surely the best thing I've ever done in my life."

Bee smiled again. Emmanuelle was struck by the impression of kindness that emanated from her. The enamel beauty of her face (which one might have thought to be free of all makeup, although Emmanuelle knew what diligence and patience had been required to produce such a perfect simulation of nature, and the many hours of skilled handling of brushes and creams), made almost embarrassing by its extreme perfection, was forgotten as soon as the playfulness shone through it, like sunlight through a stained-glass window. One then felt like saying, not "How beautiful that woman is!" but, "How likable she looks!" Emmanuelle, however, preferred to think, "How happy she seems!" She felt that this brought them closer together, because she herself was aware of being happy. And unhappiness frightened her so much that she was incapable of sincerely liking anyone who was suffering, disabled, poor, or oppressed. She was sometimes ashamed of this characteristic, although it did not stem from hard-heartedness, but only from a sensitive, almost obsessive passion for beauty.

While Marie-Anne was making conversation with the ladies, Emmanuelle stayed with Bee. They talked of nothing important, but it was clear that they both enjoyed being together. Emmanuelle was even rather glad that Marie-Anne was neglecting her. When Jean came for her, she was sorry she had to leave. As she was saying her goodbyes, Marie-Anne said, preoccupied, "I'll call you." Emmanuelle thought, too late, that she should have asked Bee for her telephone number. She was so dismayed by this oversight that she was unable to answer Jean's questions.

Without understanding exactly why, Emmanuelle dreaded seeing Ariane again. Rather than risk meeting her at the club, she gave up her morning swims. She had asked Jean what he thought of the young Countess de Saynes and he had answered that he thought she was a very pretty girl. He liked her impetuous spirit and her lack of affectation. Had he made love to her? No, but if the opportunity had arisen, he would have been glad to take it. Emmanuelle was usually rather proud of her husband's successes with other women, but this time—against all logic, since he had actually had no success with Ariane—she felt a violent pang of jealousy. She tried not to let it show, but it made the whole day seem sour.

A short time after this conversation, Ariane called to tell her that she was bored to death by the rain that had been falling for the past two days, but that she had just had a "brilliant idea." She was going to teach Emmanuelle to play squash. What was that? A kind of tennis unaffected by rain, since it was played under a roof. Emmanuelle would love it. Ariane would bring the rackets and balls; Emmanuelle would have only to change into shorts and tennis shoes and be at the club in half an hour.

She hung up before Emmanuelle had time to concoct an excuse. She had never heard of squash, but she told herself that, after all, it might be an amusing game, and she got ready with reasonably good grace.

When they met, the two women discovered that they were both dressed in the same way—yellow cotton knit shirts and black shorts. They burst out laughing.

"Are you wearing a brassiere?" inquired Ariane.

"I never wear one. I don't even own one."

"Bravo!" Ariane exclaimed enthusiastically, seizing her by the waist with both hands and lifting her slightly off the ground, much to her astonishment, for she would never have imagined that Ariane was so strong. "Don't believe a word of all those old wives' tales about tennis or horseback riding making your breasts sag if you don't tie them up in one of those straitjackets. It's just the opposite. Sports strengthen them, and the rougher you treat them the firmer they become. I can prove it. Just look at mine."

She pulled up her shirt in the middle of the terrace, as other players were passing by. Emmanuelle was not the only one who was able to admire her athletic bust.

She found that a squash court was the most ordinary thing in the world—a floor, four wooden walls, and a roof. From the gallery, it looked like a kind of pit. They went down into it by a ladder that pivoted on its topmost rung and flattened itself against the roof, automatically raised by springs as soon as they stepped off. To climb out of the pit, they would have to bring the ladder down again by pulling on a rope. Ariane explained that the game consisted of hitting a hard rubber ball against the wall with a racket that had a long handle and a small diameter.

Propelled by Ariane's smashes, the little black ball flew so fast that Emmanuelle had to run wildly from one wall to another, laughing loudly when her loose hair whipped her face. Within half an hour she was making some rather brilliant returns, but her legs were beginning to falter and she was out of breath. Her whole body was streaming with sweat. Ariane signaled for a rest and pulled the ladder down. After taking two towels from a bag that she had tied to one of the rungs, she removed her shirt and rubbed herself energetically, then she went over to Emmanuelle and wiped her chest and back with the dry towel. Emmanuelle stood still, panting. Her wet shirt was rolled up under her armpits and she felt too weary to lift her arms to take it off. Ariane backed her against the inclined ladder and she gaily pretended to let herself be crucified, spreading her arms and legs.

Ariane rubbed Emmanuelle's breasts lightly and continued long after they were dry. A not unpleasant congestion was added to the harsh sensations of breathlessness, fatigue, and thirst that were burning Emmanuelle's throat. Suddenly, Ariane dropped the towel, put her arms under Emmanuelle's, and leaned against her with her whole body. Emmanuelle felt two nipples seeking her own—as soon as they had found them, she abandoned herself to a pleasure that was too great for her to resist—and an active pubis that was pressing her through the cloth of two pairs of shorts. Her position, leaning backward, made up for her smaller height, so their mouths were on exactly the same level. Ariane kissed her as she had never been kissed before—very deeply, exploring her lips, her tongue, all the heights and hollows of her mouth, her palate, her teeth, without neglecting the slightest surface, and for so long that she never knew whether that kiss had lasted minutes or hours. She no longer felt the thirst that had been irritating her throat. She moved gently, so that her clitoris could swell, harden, and seek refuge in the solidity of the other belly. When its erection was so strong that she was like an enormous bud ready to burst, she squeezed one of Ariane's thighs between her legs, unaware of what she was doing, and began rubbing her sex against it with a lithe movement of her pelvis. Ariane let her continue for several minutes, knowing she needed that outlet for the excessive tension of her senses. Then Ariane stopped kissing her and looked at her, smiling, as she so often did, in a way that seemed to express the joy of having played a good joke on someone. Emmanuelle was embarrassed by this look and, at the same time, reassured to see that Ariane attached so little sentimentality to their intimacies. She wanted to be kissed again, and she did not want Ariane's breasts to leave her. But Ariane abruptly seized her above the hips, as she had done when they arrived, and vigorously lifted her up the ladder until her heels came to rest on one of the rungs. She thought Ariane wanted to kiss her breasts, but the tyrant kept her head at a distance and her mocking eyes never left her victim. Before Emmanuelle had time to realize clearly what was happening, Ariane's hand had slipped under her shorts and was already taking possession of her moist sex.

Her fingers were as deft, skilled, and efficient as her tongue. They grazed Emmanuelle's clitoris, then both hands, held together, plunged resolutely into the depths of her flesh, stretching the walls of her vagina and massaging the resistant protuberance of her womb with admirable animation and discernment. She let herself be drawn into orgasm without resistance, gathering her strength to make her pleasure as intense as possible, opening herself and thrusting against the hand that was probing her. She had the feeling that lava was welling up from her and flowing, thick and hot, along Ariane. When she finally slid down the ladder, unconscious, Ariane caught her in her arms and held her tightly. If she had been able to see Ariane's eyes at that moment, she might have been surprised to discover that they had lost their mocking expression.

*   *   *

By the time she came back to her senses, Ariane had regained her usual roguishness and vivacity. She was holding her by the shoulders, arms outstretched.

"Do you have enough strength left to climb up the ladder?" she asked with an affectionate laugh.

Emmanuelle was suddenly overwhelmed with embarrassment and looked down at the ground with the expression of a sulky child. Ariane took her chin between her fingers to lift it. She was again very close to her.

"Tell me," she murmured in a grave, almost choked voice that Emmanuelle had never heard before, "have other women ever done that to you?"

Emmanuelle remained outwardly impassive, but actually her mind was in a turmoil that she herself had difficulty understanding. She decided to ignore the question. Ariane insisted, however, imperious and coaxing at the same time. "Answer me. Haven't you ever made love with a woman before?"

Emmanuelle stubbornly persisted in her silence, looking like an image of false shame and sullenness. Ariane came still closer, till her lips moved against Emmanuelle's when she spoke. "Come to my house," she said thickly. "Will you?"

But Emmanuelle shook her head.

Ariane kept the rebellious chin in her hand for a long time, but she said nothing more. When at last she stepped back, there was nothing in her sprightly eyes or her mischievous pout to show whether she had been disappointed by Emmanuelle's refusal and if she was angry.

"Up you go," she said to her, after having tickled the end of her nose.

Emmanuelle turned around and climbed the ladder. Ariane followed her. Emmanuelle pulled her knit shirt, still wet, down to her waist.

"You've forgotten your shirt!" she pointed out to Ariane. "Do you want me to go down and get it for you?"

Ariane made a gesture of sovereign disdain. "Never mind, it's not worth the trouble . . . it's ruined, now."

She threw a towel around her shoulders, with no thought of covering her chest. As they walked toward the garage, she carried the rackets and her colorful cloth bag with one hand and held Emmanuelle's hand with the other. Groups of people waved to her in passing. She gaily waved back to them, uncovering her bare breasts a little more. Emmanuelle suddenly had the feeling that the whole world was looking at them. She was filled with shame and alarm. She was eager to get away from Ariane, and determined once more not to see her again.

When they reached their cars, Ariane let go of her hand, turned to face her, and finally tied the corners of the towel together, looking at her with a quizzical expression and expectation whose ironic eloquence had no need of words. Emmanuelle again bowed her head; her embarrassment and the disorder of her thoughts were not feigned. Ariane did not insist at all. She leaned forward and kissed her lightly on the cheek. "See you later, little lamb," she said blithely. She leapt into her car and drove off, waving goodbye.

When she was gone, Emmanuelle was sorry that she had done nothing to hold her back. She would have liked to see her breasts again. Above all, she would have liked to feel them on her. She suddenly wanted to be naked with Ariane lying naked on top of her, both of them very naked, more naked than they had ever been before. She wanted her breasts to be against her breasts and her sex against her sex. And she wanted to be caressed by a woman's hands, by a woman's legs, lips, body . . . Ah, if Ariane had come back at that moment, how Emmanuelle would have given herself to her!

Christopher arrived that same day. He was much more handsome than in his photographs. He had the bearing and the open smile of an English rugby player; his crudely combed blond hair seemed to be struggling against a whirlwind. Emmanuelle immediately felt at ease, as though she were with an old friend. As they were showing him around the garden, she put one arm in Jean's and the other in Christopher's.

"I won't let you make Christopher work all the time," she said to Jean, demanding her share of their guest's company in advance. "I want to take him to the *khlongs,* show him the thieves' market . . ."

"But I'm not on vacation here," protested Christopher, enchanted.

The double pleasure of seeing Jean again and discovering how happily married he was made that Sunday a glorious occasion for him. He did not hide the admiration Emmanu-elle aroused in him.

"That scoundrel Jean is really too lucky," he exclaimed, giving her an enthusiastic look. "He hasn't done anything to deserve this!"

"I'm glad he hasn't," she said jokingly. "I couldn't stand a deserving husband!"

They stayed up late, joyful and noisy; they did not go to bed until sleep triumphed over Emmanuelle, closing her eyes as she sat curled up in an armchair under the bougainvillaea that covered the ground-floor terrace. It was not raining. The bullfrogs had fallen silent. The stars had their dry-season color. The middle of August often offers such deceptive respites.

Emmanuelle slept naked, but before going out to have break-fast with Jean on the wide balcony of their bedroom she some-times put on one of the very short little nightgowns that she bought—partly for the pleasure of trying them on—before leaving Paris. The one she was wearing this morning was transparent, pleated, and almost the same color as her skin. The hem came down only to her groin. Three buttons held it closed at the waist. The slightest breath of air lifted it. She sud-denly laughed. "Good heavens, I'd forgotten we have a guest! I'd better put on something a little more decent."

Jean intervened as she was about to leave. "Absolutely not," he decreed, "you look much better this way."

She had no objection, actually, to showing herself in that attire, because she had long been accustomed to being seen naked by all sorts of people. In that respect, Jean's attitude was a continuation of her parents'. The idea that she ought to put on a dressing gown before appearing in front of them would have seemed as absurd to them as to her. She had bought her nightgowns after her marriage out of coquettishness, not out of modesty.

Christopher was less at ease than his hosts. Sitting opposite Emmanuelle, he could not take his eyes off her breasts, animated by the sunlight shining through the pleats, with their nipples like two spots of blood. When she stood up to bring him biscuits, fruit, and honey, the morning breeze parted her airy gown to her navel, and her astrakhan triangle came so close to his face that he could smell its lily-of-the-valley fragrance.

He did not dare to raise his cup of tea to his lips, for fear his hands might tremble. "What will become of me if I have to stand up?" he thought, panic-stricken. "Or if someone comes to remove the table cloth?"

Emmanuelle fortunately went back into her bedroom before the men had finished eating. Christopher thus had time to recover his self-control.

They were not going to return till dinner. Emmanuelle did not feel like staying home alone all day. She got into her car and went to the center of the city. For an hour she drove around aimlessly, often getting lost, stopping sometimes to go into a store. Once she was frozen in horrified contemplation of a leper. Sitting on the sidewalk, he was moving backward, supporting himself on his decomposing wrists and dragging the stumps of his thighs along the soiled ground. She was so shaken by the sight that she was unable to start the engine of her car. She sat there paralyzed, having forgotten where she wanted to go and the movements she had to make, with her undecayed feet, her healthy, fragile hands . . . Just then she saw someone she recognized coming out of a Chinese shop not far away. She shouted, as though calling for help: "Bee!"

Bee turned around, made a gesture of joyful surprise, and walked over to the car.

"I've been looking for you," said Emmanuelle. And as soon as she said it, she realized that it was true.

"Well, you're lucky to have found me," Bee said with amusement, "because I don't come here often."

"Naturally she doesn't believe me," Emmanuelle thought sadly. "Would you like to have lunch with me?" she asked so imploringly that for a moment Bee did not know what to answer. It was Emmanuelle who broke the silence: "I've got an idea! Come home with me. There are plenty of things to eat. And you haven't seen my house yet."

"Wouldn't you rather try some of the local specialties? There's a very picturesque little restaurant near here. Let me take you to lunch there."

"No, no!" Emmanuelle said stubbornly. "Some other time. Now that I've found you, I want you to come home with me."

"If you like." Bee opened the door of the car and sat down beside her.

Emmanuelle blossomed. She suddenly had the feeling of having found herself again, sure of her desires, proud of what she loved, as incapable of pretending as of waiting. She stopped just short of shouting out her joy at the top of her lungs as she drove through the anthill of the city, scorning all caution. She laughed loudly, without a pretext. She seemed to give off rays of light.

Bee looked at her with admiration and a little apprehension.

The elegance and modern interior decor of the house pleased Bee. She praised the flower arrangements, a Japanese talent that Emmanuelle had acquired in Paris; she praised the ceramic furniture, the basins of translucent stone adorned with coral and seashells, and the big wrought-iron mobile that stood in the middle of the room, cumbersome, provocative, rattling with all its bizarre metal foliage.

They ate lunch rapidly. Emmanuelle had lost the power of speech. Her jubilant gaze never left Bee.

Then they visited the garden, despite the burning sun. Emmanuelle guided Bee by the hand through its slips and cuttings. They imagined the beauty of its landscape once its shrubbery would be in bloom.

She plucked a long-stemmed rose and handed it to Bee, who put her fingers around the red corolla and held it against her cheek. Emmanuelle moved her lips forward and kissed the rose.

By the time they went back into the house, sweat was flowing down their faces and necks.

"Shall we take a shower?" Emmanuelle suggested.

Bee acknowledged that it was a good idea.

As soon as they were in her bedroom, Emmanuelle pulled off her clothes as hastily as if they had been on fire. Bee did not begin undressing until Emmanuelle had taken off her last garment. First she said, "What a beautiful body you have!" Then she slowly unbuttoned her collar. When she opened her blouse, which she, too, wore directly over her skin, Emmanuelle could not but notice that Bee's chest was like a boy's.

"You see how flat I am," she said. She did not seem at all humiliated. She enjoyed Emmanuelle's surprise as she inspected the pink nipples, so small and pale that they seemed prepubescent.

"Do you think it's ugly?" she asked without much seriousness.

"Oh, no! It's wonderful!" Emmanuelle cried out so fervently that Bee seemed touched.

"You have a right to be critical if you want to. Your own breasts are magnificent. We form a startling contrast, don't we?"

But Emmanuelle was now a convert and a fanatic. "What's so interesting about having big breasts? That's all you ever see on magazine covers. But with you, it's so different from other women! It's so pretty!" Her voice softened a little. "I've never seen anything so exciting, really . . . I mean what I say."

"I admit I find it rather amusing," said Bee, taking off her skirt. "I don't think I'd like to have breasts that were too little, but there's a certain humor in not having any breasts at all, don't you agree?" She suddenly seemed more loquacious; Emmanuelle could not remember having heard her make so long a speech before. "For a long time, in fact, I lived in dread of seeing my breasts begin to grow. It would have made me feel as if I'd lost all my personality. And I prayed every night, 'Dear God, please let me never have real breasts.' I was so good that God gave me my wish!"

"What luck!" exclaimed Emmanuelle. "It would have been terrible if your breasts had grown. I like you so much this way!"

She also felt that Bee had admirable legs, so long and with such pure lines that they belonged in a fashion drawing and did not seem quite real. Her narrow hips and the flexible slenderness of her waist added to the impression of aristocratic elegance. But what struck Emmanuelle still more was the extraordinarily protruding shaved pubis that appeared when Bee had taken off her panties. She had never seen one that stood out so prominently, or was so swollen with female sexuality. She told herself that she knew nothing in the world more beautiful or worthier of being loved. The absence of hair revealed the slit of Bee's sex, which rose high and was deeply and sharply cut, offering itself to the spectator's gaze without ambiguity. There was a kind of defiance in the fact that her boyish chest was tanned the same as the rest of her body, so that one could not help assuming that it had also been exposed to the sun and that others had been able to contemplate that hermaphroditic nudity at leisure. And, despite her distant grace, the smooth, split bulge at the bottom of her belly was so sensual, and thrust itself forward so invitingly, that Emmanuelle felt as if her own sex were being probed by a hand. She knew she had to possess Bee without delay; that voluptuous furrow, that crack, had to be opened to her . . . Oh, that crack! The sight of it made her tremble. She opened her mouth to say what she wanted, but just then Bee turned toward the bathroom.

"What about that shower?" she asked.

The artifice now seemed superfluous to Emmanuelle. "Come to bed," she ordered, to cut Bee's movement short.

Bee stopped in front of the door, hesitantly. Then she made up her mind to laugh. "But I feel like cooling off, not sleeping," she said.

Emmanuelle wondered if she really thought she had been invited to take a nap, or if she was only pretending innocence. Looking at her as she stood there naked, she was dismayed to see no veiled meaning in her eyes.

She went over to Bee and opened the door. "Then we'll make love in the shower," she said firmly.

4

Cavatina,
or the Love of Bee

Stop, moment: thou art so beautiful!
—Johann Wolfgang von Goethe, *Faust*

I shall leave the bed as she left it, unmade and disrupted,
with the sheets tangled, so that the form of her body
will remain imprinted beside mine.
Until tomorrow, I shall not go to the bath, I shall wear no
garments and I shall not comb my hair, lest I efface her caresses.
I shall not eat this morning, nor this evening, and on my lips
I shall put neither rouge nor powder, so that her kiss will remain.
I shall leave the shutters closed and I shall not open the door,
lest the lingering memory be carried away by the wind.
—Pierre Louÿs, *Les Chansons de Bilitis*,
"Le passé qui survit"

The big white bathroom was equipped with several kinds of showers. One was attached to the ceiling, another to the wall, a third and smaller one at the end of a long, flexible tube that could be held in the hand and bent in any direction. The two women stood beside each other under the crossed streams of water. Emmanuelle had drawn her hair up to the top of her head to protect it, and that made her look as tall as Bee.

She told Bee that she was going to show her how to use the flexible shower. She took the tube in her right hand, put her left arm around Bee's hips, and ordered her to spread her legs.

Bee smiled and obeyed. Emmanuelle sent the warm jet slanting downward to Bee's sex, then moved it closer, sometimes making it quiver slightly, sometimes giving it a spiral motion. She seemed thoroughly familiar with the rules of that game. The water cascaded between Bee's legs. Emmanuelle looked up. "Does it feel good?" she asked.

Bee seemed to consider the question incongruous. She hesitated a moment, apparently wanting to say something, then she changed her mind and finally contented herself with nodding. A moment later, however, she admitted, "Yes, very good."

Without ceasing to direct the shower with a sure hand, Emmanuelle leaned forward and took one of Bee's little nipples in her mouth. She felt a hand touch her hair. Was it to push her away? Was it to draw her closer? She pressed the miniature bud between her lips, provoked it with the tip of her tongue, sucked it. It immediately became hard and more than doubled its size. She lifted her head, triumphantly. "You see . . ."

She stopped short. Bee's features had lost their mask of serenity. Her gray eyes were still more immense, her lips were thicker and more lustrous. With her face almost childlike, purified, a Bee whom Emmanuelle had not known till now, electrifyingly intense and beautiful, abandoned herself to orgasm without a cry, without a quiver, without letting the rhythm of her body betray the violence of her pleasure.

Her ecstasy continued so long that Emmanuelle wondered if she was still aware of her presence. Then, little by little, her marvelous expression faded away and Emmanuelle was sad that her sensual rapture could not have lasted forever. She was so intimidated by the transfiguration she had witnessed that she did not dare to speak. Bee smiled at her.

Emmanuelle put her arms around her neck and kissed her lips. She moaned with pleasure when Bee's body fused with hers. The streaming coolness of their two skins was a caress in itself. She embraced her tightly and slowly rubbed her pubis against hers.

Bee sensed the pleasure that Emmanuelle was seeking; she put her hand on her back, pressed gently on her buttocks, and grafted her onto her belly. A singular savor penetrated her open mouth, juicy and sweet like an exotic fruit. She felt a spasm rising in the beautiful body she was holding against herself. She helped it with all her power. She heard her lips murmuring words that had the sound of love.

"Emmanuelle is intelligent, curious about everything, and always in a good humor, but that's not why I married her," Jean said to Christopher as the jeep rolled along, making two red ruts on the slimy road.

Their skin was sticky with sweat, the heaviness of the air inflamed their throats. They crossed a little bridge. Naked boys and girls were playing in the water, splashing each other amid shouts of laughter.

"Look. Isn't that the Orient you see in films?"

Jean stopped the engine. They went down to the stream and cooled their faces. The children leaped with enthusiasm, pointing at them, and chirping in chorus, *"Farang! Farang!"*

"What are they saying?" Christopher asked uneasily.

"Only 'Europeans! Europeans!' The way European children shout, 'Chinese! Chinese!'"

A little girl, whose wet hair caressed her shoulders with long black tongues, came over to them. She had picked up a bright, blue sarong, which contrasted with the amber of her skin, and was tying it around her waist as she walked.

"Than yak sue som-o mai tja?" she asked, giving the foreigners a bewitching smile.

"I don't know what she wants," Jean confessed to Christopher.

She pointed to a basket of enormous grapefruit that had been placed in the shade of a breadfruit tree.

"Ah, I see. She's offering us some grapefruit. That's not a bad idea."

Jean nodded and said, *"Ao ko dai!"*

The girl ran over to the basket and came back with a grapefruit bigger than her head. She held up a hand with all five fingers spread apart.

"Ha baht."

"It's a deal," said Jean. He handed her a five-baht note which she examined carefully. "There, are our accounts in order?"

"Kha!"

She seemed to take this bilingual conversation in stride. Christopher was surprised.

"Does she understand French?"

"Not a single word. But that doesn't mean we can't have a little chat."

She held the fruit up to her face with a questioning expression.

"Pok hai mai tja?"

Jean spread his arms in a gesture of incomprehension. The girl's free hand drew imaginary rings around the grainy skin of the fruit, then went through the motions of peeling it.

"Yes, of course, why not?" said Jean. "That would be nice of you."

She went back to her basket, took out a little knife with a sharp, curved, bronze blade, and sat down with the grapefruit on her skirt, which was pulled tight by her crossed legs.

The two men sat down on the grass, facing her.

"Since you didn't marry Emmanuelle for her mind, as you've said, I suppose it must have been for her beauty," said Christopher, returning to their earlier conversation. "That's easy to understand."

"Maybe, but her beauty wouldn't have been enough to conquer me."

"What did, then? Her household talents?"

"No, her carnal genius. I don't know anyone in the world who likes to make love as much as she does. Or who does it as well."

Christopher was shocked. This kind of confidence seemed to him in bad taste. But he was eager to hear more. "You're lucky, of course," he said with a certain effort, "but aren't you also running a risk? That . . . what do you call it? . . . that gift she has . . . others may sense it . . . They may be tempted to . . . try to take advantage of it . . . take her away from you."

"No one can take something away from me that doesn't belong to me," Jean said as if this were self-evident. "She's not my property. She's not my beauty."

Christopher was puzzled.

"I didn't marry her to own her," Jean added.

The little girl held out several grapefruit sections, on her joined palms. Jean accepted one, after nodding his thanks, and ate it with obvious pleasure.

"Don't you want any?" he asked Christopher.

Christopher mechanically took some of the offered fruit, staring at the scene with an absent-minded look.

"Emmanuelle and I are interested in the world," Jean went on. "And we both have a desire to know more about it." He laughed and remarked zestfully, "There's plenty to do!" He took two grapefruit sections from the girl's hands. "Even for the two of us. And enough to justify teamwork."

Christopher wondered if Jean's words had any connection with his own question. The children had squatted in a circle around them and were now watching them in silence, though from time to time they nudged each other and burst into wild laughter that brought tears to their eyes.

"They seem to be making fun of us," remarked Christopher. The fruit had refreshed his tongue, but his throat remained curiously tight. He tried to struggle against the images that imposed themselves on his mind with gentle insistence and horrified him. "That's no way to think of a friend's wife!" he told himself.

The vision persisted just the same. He suggested, in a false voice, that they buy another grapefruit. But while the little girl was preparing it for them and he was forcing himself to talk about canal locks and kilowatts, his imagination tirelessly re-created Emmanuelle's round breasts, her muscular buttocks, the tempting nakedness of her belly . . . Jean leaped to his feet and announced that it was time for them to be on their way. Only then did he notice Christopher's state of excitement, spectacular under his thin, white, twill shorts. He rounded his lips in surprise and laughed.

"I didn't know you had such tastes!" he said jubilantly. "I won't introduce you to any more little girls." He mockingly called Christopher's condition to the attention of their hostess, who did not seem at all offended. "Listen, you should at least wait until they're a little less green. This one can't be more than eight years old!"

* * *

Emmanuelle began lathering Bee's body. She knew how to go about it so well, slipping her hand between Bee's legs, that Bee had to defend herself.

"No, no, not all the time, Emmanuelle! It's too tiring. Let me get some of my strength back."

Emmanuelle let her rinse and dry herself, then she said cajolingly, "Come into my bed!"

Bee made no reply and Emmanuelle immediately became panic-stricken. Bee kissed her on the eyelids.

"Let's go to your bedroom," she said.

Emmanuelle pushed her down across the big bed, lay on top of her, covered her forehead, cheeks, and neck with kisses, nibbled her ear lobes and her bosom. She slid down to the floor, knelt, and buried her face in Bee's bare belly.

"Oh," she moaned, "how soft!" She rubbed her cheeks, her nose, and her lips against the elastic bulge of Bee's pubis. "Darling! Darling!"

Bee remained motionless and silent.

"Are you happy like this?" Emmanuelle asked anxiously.

"Yes."

"You're willing, aren't you? Willing to let me love you?"

"But, Emmanuelle . . ." Bee stopped short, caressed Emmanuelle's loose hair, and waited.

Emmanuelle's hands pushed her long legs apart, grazed the opening that separated them and gently penetrated it.

Bee sighed, let her arms fall along her sides, and closed her eyes. Emmanuelle moved the tip of her tongue toward Bee's sex, narrow and smooth as a virgin's. She moistened the edges of her vulva, licked it inside, then sought her clitoris, drew it into her mouth, stimulated it with vibrations, softened it with saliva, made it move back and forth between her lips like a miniature penis. She slipped her bent middle finger into her own vagina. She continued stimulating Bee's sex with her free hand. Her fingers were wet. She ran them over Bee's buttocks, which rose to let her penetrate the narrow orifice. Her finger sank in to its full length. Only then did Bee cry out, and she continued during the whole time while Emmanuelle was licking her, sucking her, and moving her hand from one opening of her body to another. It was Emmanuelle who first had to admit that she was tired. She lay down on Bee again. Neither of them seemed to have the strength to speak.

Later, when Bee had put on her clothes despite Emmanuelle's pleas, Emmanuelle put her arms around her neck and made her sit down on the bed.

"I want you to tell me something. But promise me it will be the truth!"

Bee answered only with an affirmative smile.

"I love you," said Emmanuelle.

Bee looked into the depths of her golden eyes, trying to determine what reply she was supposed to give, what kind of truth was expected of her. But Emmanuelle's grave, almost tragic expression had already given way to a winsome pout. She put her cheek on Bee's shoulder.

"Are you sure I please you? I mean . . . no, wait . . . listen to me first . . . do I please you as much as, or more than, any of your other friends? Did I give you as much pleasure?"

This time Bee laughed. Emmanuelle took offense. "Why are you making fun of me?" she complained.

"Listen, my little Emmanuelle," murmured Bee, moving close to her lips, "I'm going to tell you a big secret. I never did this before."

"You mean the shower, the . . ."

"Everything! I've never made love, as you put it, with another woman."

"Oh, I don't believe you!" protested Emmanuelle, frowning.

"You have to believe me, because it's true. And I'm going to admit something else to you. Until this afternoon, until I knew you, I even thought it was a little ridiculous."

"But . . ." stammered Emmanuelle, taken aback. "Do you mean you never liked it?"

"I never liked or disliked it, since I hadn't tried it."

"That's impossible!" Emmanuelle exclaimed in a way that made Bee laugh.

"Why? Did I seem like such an expert to you?" Bee asked in a tone of almost bantering complicity that was new to Emmanuelle and disconcerted her.

"You didn't seem surprised."

"I wasn't. Because it was you."

"Oh?" said Emmanuelle. She reflected for a moment, then asked as though she were coming out of a dream, as though she had forgotten everything that had been said before, "Don't you love me, Bee?"

Bee looked at her without smiling. "I'm very fond of you, yes."

Emmanuelle had expected something else. She asked another question, less because it was important to her than because she wanted to break the silence. "Did . . . did you like the experience? Are you happy?"

Bee seemed to make up her mind abruptly. "This time," she said, "*I'm* going to caress *you*."

Emmanuelle did not have time to answer. Bee firmly took her by the waist, forcing her to lie down, and kissed her sex as though it were her mouth, turning her head sideways so that her own lips would be parallel to those other lips. She put out her tongue and slipped it into the docile furrow as far as she could. All at once Emmanuelle felt herself submerged in both love and sensuality. Surprised by this sudden orgasm before she had been able to try any other caresses, Bee quickly drew back, but when she saw that Emmanuelle was still being shaken by convulsive tremors, she applied her mouth again and scrupulously licked away the juice that was flowing from her. When she raised her head she said, laughing, "I never would have thought that some day I'd like to drink from that spring! Well, as you can see, now I do like it!"

The ringing of the telephone bell broke the spell. It was Marie-Anne, calling to say that she was about to come for a visit. Ordinarily, this would have delighted Emmanuelle, but now it threw her into consternation. It took all of Bee's good humor to calm her. Neither of them cared to confront Marie-Anne together, so they agreed to see each other again the next day. Bee would come to Emmanuelle's house in the morning. The chauffeur took her home.

Emmanuelle waited for Marie-Anne without bothering to put on any clothes. The surprising part of it was that she had no thought, at that time, of trying to approach her little friend.

She was incapable of disguising her emotions enough to prevent Marie-Anne's perspicacity from immediately putting her on the alert.

"What's happened to you? You look like a girl who's just been proposed to."

"I've got some big news that will interest you."

"You're pregnant?"

"Idiot!

"Tell me, what have you done?"

"I've made love with Bee."

She made this revelation without being at all sure of the effect it would produce. Even so, she did not expect Marie-Anne's reaction to be so discouraging.

"Is that all?" she asked jadedly. "It didn't deserve all those preliminaries. What's so amazing about it?"

"But . . ." said Emmanuelle, thrown off balance. "Bee is fascinating! Wouldn't you find her to your taste, by any chance?"

Marie-Anne shrugged.

"Poor Emmanuelle, you're such a half-wit. I really don't see what glory there can be in going to bed with a girl. You announce it as if it were a great achievement—you make me laugh!"

Emmanuelle was embarrassed. Furthermore, she was beginning to feel guilty. But of what? She tried to see things more clearly.

"What have you got against the fact that Bee and I have made love?"

Marie-Anne's verdict had a definitive sound. "You don't make love with a woman."

"Oh?"

"You make love with a man," said Marie-Anne. "If you don't know that yet," she went on in a tone of impatient authority, "I know someone who can teach it to you, as I've already told you. Since words apparently have no effect on you, I'd better turn you over to Mario right away." She seemed to be mentally consulting a calendar. "Today is the sixteenth. You're invited to the Embassy on the eighteenth, aren't you? Good. I'll introduce him to you at that reception. If you can't manage to make love with him that same night, it will have to be the next day."

She could not bear to go on waiting much longer. She was kneeling on an armchair on the balcony of her bedroom, with her elbows on the railing and her chin in her hands, scrutinizing the street through the foliage of the garden. Anxiety made her lips quiver. Would she come? Why was she so late? Maybe she would find an excuse for not coming. Emmanuelle dreaded hearing the telephone ring.

It was she, however, who decided to call, when hours had gone by and waiting had become too painful. It was nearly noon. A man's voice answered when she dialed the number that Bee had given her. A servant, probably. Only then did she realize that she could not ask about Bee, not only because she was unable to speak the local language, but also because she did not even know her real name. Could she refer to her by a nickname to a servant? She tried it, but could not tell whether or not she had been understood. She gave up.

Since Bee herself had not answered, it might mean that she was on her way. If so, she was going to arrive at any moment. Emmanuelle went back to her observation post. Could there have been an accident? Perhaps Bee had been unable to find her house again, and had been wandering for hours in search of it, through the labyrinth of residential quarters. All the streets looked alike and their names were not only unpronounceable but also written in Thai characters, so it would not be surprising if Bee had gotten lost.

But after all, objected a voice that was stronger than Emmanuelle's hope, Bee had been living in Bangkok for a year, long enough to learn to find her way around. Emmanuelle was doing fairly well after only two weeks. How could she believe that Bee had lost her way? At most she might be a little delayed. And she should have arrived two hours ago. If she had forgotten where Emmanuelle lived, what was to prevent her from telephoning, or asking her to come and get her?

Why not go to Bee's house? She immediately realized that she had neglected to ask her for her address. Marie-Anne had said she was the sister of an American naval attaché. That was a little vague. In any case, Emmanuelle was not going to call the American Embassy for information. On second thought, why not? But, once again, what name could she ask for? There might be several naval attachés. And in what language would she ask?

The chauffeur! He had taken Bee home the day before! Emmanuelle sent for him, trembling with impatience. He could not be found anywhere. He had no doubt gone out to lunch. Or to play dice.

How stupid she was! Why hadn't she thought of it sooner? She had only to call Marie-Anne. But as soon as she had the idea she had second thoughts. Could she admit to that greeneyed little girl that she was waiting for Bee, and thus expose herself to more sarcasm? Above all, her wounded pride advised her against letting Marie-Anne guess that Bee had failed to show up, that perhaps she did not share Emmanuelle's amorous fervor, and that the tender mistress of the day before had already become fickle.

Emmanuelle was now sure that Bee would not come. She would not come later in the afternoon, or the next day. She had yielded, the day before, to an enchantment stronger than she was, but now that she was away from Emmanuelle she had regained her self-control, she did not love her, she did not like women, that game seemed absurd and boring to her, she had judged herself "ridiculous" afterward, to use her own word. Or else she was ashamed of having let herself be drawn into the pleasures of the flesh. Emmanuelle told herself that Bee might have religious beliefs or a concept of morality that had made her repent the debauchery to which she had abandoned herself. After all, Emmanuelle knew nothing about her. She probably did not have a lover, since she lived with her brother, and it was all too certain that she did not have a mistress.

Unless . . . The opposite hypothesis took its turn in Emmanuelle's mind. Did Bee actually have another mistress? Maybe she had lied the day before. No, that was one thing Emmanuelle could not believe. A lover, then? Had she admitted her "unfaithfulness" to him? Had he made a jealous scene and demanded that she never see her accomplice again? That was it, Emmanuelle was convinced. But she would not let herself be ousted so easily! She would fight to win Bee back; she had the strength of love . . .

A moment later, she felt only weakness and suffering. An unknown bitterness was gradually submerging all the confidence she had left, everything in her that refused to surrender. Bee would never come back, she did not want to see her again. Her reasons didn't matter. Nothing mattered but Emmanuelle's abandonment and solitude. She loved her so much! She had the feeling that she had come to that country at the end of the world only to find Bee. She had recognized her at first sight as the one she had always been waiting for. She would have gone with her wherever she might have chosen to take her. She would have given up everything for her, if that had been her will. But Bee would ask for nothing. And Emmanuelle would never again, never, offer her what she had been ready to give her. Yes, she would erase her from her memory! She would forget her stained-glass face and her hair of fire, she would forget the muffled voice that had said to her, "I'm very fond of you, yes."

For the first time since childhood, real tears, long tears, flowed down her face, wetting her lips and salting her tongue, falling on the balustrade of the terrace, which she could not bring herself to leave. She wept as one stretches out one's arms—vainly facing the opening in the foliage where, in a moment, that evening, perhaps the next day, at any time, whenever she saw fit, Bee would appear and wave to her . . .

That evening, Jean and Christopher took her to the theater. She did not know what she was seeing. Her face declared her grief. Jean did not question her; Christopher, who understood nothing of what was happening, looked almost as sad as Emmanuelle. Later, when she was in Jean's arms, in their bed, she again wept her fill. She felt somewhat relieved. She was less heartbroken when she confessed her unhappy love to him.

It was his opinion that she was taking the adventure too tragically. In the first place, there was no proof that Bee's absence had not been due to fortuitous circumstances and that she would not appear the next day with a perfectly valid excuse. If, however, it turned out that she did not want to see Emmanuelle again, it would mean only that she was not worth all the anxiety that Emmanuelle was feeling. It would be better if their affair ended immediately, because it would surely bring her nothing but more serious disappointments and sorrows. In any case, she ought to think of herself as someone whom others ran after, not as someone who ran after others. Jean had never seen Bee, or even heard of her until now, but no matter how beautiful she might be, he was certain that she had only a small fraction of Emmanuelle's charm and merit. He would therefore not permit Emmanuelle to humiliate herself before Bee. The only answer her faithless mistress deserved, if she thought she could be grudging with her favors, was for Emmanuelle to take her revenge in other arms. She would have no trouble finding partners worthier of her. She owed it to herself to prove it to Bee without delay.

She listened to him docilely. "He's right," she thought. Her pain was not really assuaged, but listening to someone else talk to her about consoling herself or taking revenge, she was somewhat distracted from her distress. It already seemed less distinct to her. Perhaps it was only because she was sleepy. She never knew whether her last thought, before losing consciousness, had been of her fugitive mistress or of the other women, still faceless, who would replace her some day.

Jean had told Emmanuelle that none of the dresses she had bought in France was cut low enough to suit him.

"But there's no woman in Paris who shows her breasts as much as I do!" she had protested, laughing.

"What Paris calls showing one's breasts is still too strait-laced for Bangkok," Jean had answered. "All those people must know for certain that you have the most beautiful bosom in the world, and the surest way to convince them of it is to display it in front of their eyes."

The dress that Emmanuelle put on to go to the reception at the French Embassy was perfectly adapted to this purpose. Its round neckline, which clung to the slope of her shoulders, enhanced, by its broad curve, the beauty of her neck, and covered only the tips of her breasts. All she had to do to make them appear completely was to lean forward a little, or sit down. Furthermore, the lamé cloth was so thin and so tight against her skin that any undergarment would have shown through or been outlined in relief, so she was wearing nothing under that dress, not even a pair of her diaphanous panties. In Paris, after her marriage, she had seldom worn panties when she "dressed up" to go out in the evening; feeling naked in that way gave her a pleasure as physical as a caress. This sensation was still more intense if she was going to dance, or if she was wearing a loose skirt.

This evening, her dress fitted her as tightly as a glove from her waist to her groin, but below this point it abruptly flared out in a kind of spiral whose fullness was surprising. She let herself fall into an armchair to show how the skirt rose of its own accord, revealing the whole length of her golden thighs. The sight she thus offered was so gracefully immodest that Jean suddenly leaned down, reached for the invisible nylon zipper under her armpit, and pulled it down to the bottom of her hip with a sure hand while, with the other, he tried to free her nude body from its silk sheath.

"Jean," she protested, "what are you doing? Have you lost your mind? We'll be late! We have to leave right now!"

He gave up trying to undress her. He picked her up and stretched her out on the table in the dining room.

"No! Oh, no! My dress will be all wrinkled. You're hurting me! What if Christopher comes in? The servants will see us!"

He placed her on her back so that her buttocks were just touching the edge of the table. She herself pulled up her skirt to uncover her belly as much as possible. Her raised, half-bent legs were suspended in the air. Jean, standing, penetrated her all at once, completely. They were both laughing at this impromptu scene. His haste gave her a new pleasure that made her throat burn as if she had been running. She pressed her breasts with her hands, as though to squeeze out their nectar. Her own caresses inflamed her as much as Jean's furious lunges. At her first cries, the houseboy hurried into the room, thinking she had called him. He stopped hesitantly in the doorway with his hands crossed politely over his chest. It must have been possible to hear her from the houses near by.

When Jean had put her back on her feet, he told the houseboy to clean the table, which they had spotted, and to call Ea, Emmanuelle's little chambermaid, so that she could help her put her appearance in order again. They arrived at the Embassy a little late.

The crowd was already large. The ambassador, having reached the end of his stay, was giving a farewell reception.

"Ravishing!" he said appreciatively, before kissing Emmanuelle's hand. He turned to Jean. "Congratulations, my friend! I hope your work leaves you some free time."

A white-haired lady, to whom Emmanuelle recalled having paid a visit, was staring at her with an expression of wrathful disapproval. Ariane de Saynes arrived in time to make things worse.

"Why, if I'm not mistaken," she cried, holding out both her hands, "here's our living outrage to public decency! Let's hurry and give her a fair trial!" She attracted the attention of an elegant man who was conversing with a bishop. "Look, Gilbert! What do you think of her?"

Emmanuelle felt herself being appraised by the Embassy Counselor and the cleric at the same time. She felt that she was doing better with the former than with the latter. She had more or less expected Ariane's husband to be a kind of pompous, monocle-wearing simpleton. But the first words he said made her laugh loudly, and she found him physically very much to her taste.

She was already surrounded by gentlemen of various ages who were paying her gallant compliments and giving her obvious looks, but her attention was distracted; she was studying the unknown faces in the distance, both wishing and dreading that she would find Bee. The whole diplomatic corps was to be present. Could Bee's brother have been invited without her? Maybe so. Emmanuelle did not know what her attitude would be if she should suddenly find herself face to face with the American girl. She hoped with all her strength that she would not meet her. Each group seemed to hide a trap. What was she doing here? When would she be able to escape, or at least be under Jean's protection again? He had been swallowed up in the crowd.

Ariane reappeared opportunely to take charge of her and dragged her into a whirlwind of introductions. The admiration of the men followed her everywhere. This homage, to which she was accustomed, restored her self-assurance. Her face pretended indifference, but all those eyes that undressed her warmed her at least as much as the cocktails that Ariane poured into her.

Ariane silently watched Emmanuelle joust with a quartet of aviators, holding her shoulders forward and tilting her bust a little. She abruptly drew her aside.

"You're magnificent!" she exclaimed. Her eyes were flashing. She delicately took the tip of one of Emmanuelle's enticing breasts between her fingers. "Come with me," she urged. "In that drawing room back there . . . it's empty!"

"No, no!" Emmanuelle said rebelliously.

Before Ariane could stop her, she hurried back to the mass of guests and did not feel safe until an aging gentleman had taken her to the edge of the terrace, on the pretext of letting her admire the Chinese lanterns made of painted pigs' bladders. Marie-Anne discovered her while she was still talking with him.

"Excuse me, Commander," she said with her usual aplomb, "I have to speak to my friend."

She took Emmanuelle's arm, ignoring the graybeard's protests.

"What were you doing with that old fogey?" she said indignantly as soon as they had taken a few steps. "I've been looking for you everywhere. Mario has been waiting half an hour for you."

Emmanuelle had forgotten this rendezvous. She was not in the mood for it. While the old man had been paying court to her, she had at least been able to think about other things in peace and quiet. She tried to plead for her freedom.

"Is it really necessary?"

"Now listen, Emmanuelle!" Marie-Anne said with exasperation. "Wait till you see him before you start acting so difficult!"

She sounded so comically promising that Emmanuelle regained her good humor. Before she had time to deride Marie-Anne's confidence in her hero's charms, he was standing in front of her.

"What a beautiful smile!" he said, bowing. "How I wish it could have served as a model for the painters of my country! Don't you find that those restrained smiles, those Florentine intimations, eventually begin to seem like grimaces? They refuse art. I reject everything that contains itself. After all those centuries of grudgingly doling out the favors of its statues, art still exists in its truth only in a candid face."

Emmanuelle was a bit taken aback by this conversational beginning.

"Marie-Anne insists on having me painted." (She reflected that Marie-Anne had not even bothered to introduce them.) "Are you the artist she considers worthy of the task?"

Mario smiled. She inwardly admitted that his smile had a rare charm.

"If I had only a hundredth of the talent that I permit myself to challenge in others, Madame, I would offer it to you; the genius of the model would do the rest. Unfortunately, I lack even that. I'm rich only in the art of others."

Marie-Anne intervened. "He's a collector, wait till you see! In his house he has not only sculpture from here, but ancient things he brought from Mexico, Africa, and Greece. And paintings . . ."

"Which have no value but to serve as motionless reminders of true art, whose risk and movement defy dead figures. Marie-Anne *mia,* I don't believe in those scraps of bark fallen from the tree of life. I keep them only in memory of those who have suffered and destroyed themselves to tear them from its trunk or its branches. Art is made of the wasting away of being. What counts is not the painting—as in Poe's 'The Oval Portrait'—but the painter's bride."

"Once she's dead?" asked Emmanuelle.

"No, while she's dying."

"But hasn't the painting become alive?"

"Nonsense! It's nothing but a shoddy curiosity. Art existed only in what was being lost, in the woman who was deteriorating. There can be no beauty in what maintains itself or in what subsists. Every conceived object is stillborn."

"I was taught the opposite—that only robust art has eternity . . ."

"And would you please tell me who cares about eternity?" Mario interrupted violently. "Eternity is not artistic, it's ugly; its face is that of a monument to the dead. Every memorial is another corpse in the city. If you try to make beauty eternal, it dies. What's beautiful is not what's bare, but what's baring itself. Not the sound of laughter, but the throat that's laughing. Not what's left on paper, but the moment when the artist's heart is being torn."

"You said just now that the artist was less important than the model."

"The sculptor or the painter is the artist only if he takes hold of his subject and *unmakes* it. But often the model fulfills that destiny unaided, and the painter is only a witness. Allow me to quote Miguel de Unamuno: 'The greatest work of art is not worth the smallest human life.' The only art that's not futile is the story of your body."

"Do you mean that what matters is the way you create yourself? That you have to conceive of yourself as a work of art if you want to live beyond yourself?"

"No," said Mario, "I don't believe any such thing . . . If I had any right to give you advice," he said with faintly disdainful courtesy, "I'd urge you not to live beyond yourself, but just to live."

He turned away. He seemed to consider that the conversation was over. Emmanuelle felt that her presence was no longer required. It was a rather disagreeable feeling. She spoke to Marie-Anne with a touch of ill-humor: "You haven't seen Jean by any chance, have you? He vanished as soon as we got here."

Other women monopolized the Italian; Emmanuelle took advantage of the interruption to slip away. But Marie-Anne quickly rejoined her.

"Are you keeping Bee under lock and key?" she asked, without giving the impression that she attached much importance to her question. "Every time I try to call her, I'm told that she's at your house." She gave a rather good-natured little laugh. "And since I don't want to disturb your love life . . ."

Emmanuelle was dumbfounded. Was Marie-Anne making fun of her? No, she seemed to believe what she was saying. What irony! Emmanuelle was on the verge of complaining aloud. Once again, she was restrained by fear of what Marie-Anne would think. Could she admit to her that she had lost all trace of her one-day mistress? It would be better to maintain the illusions that the little girl in pigtails still had about her elder's power. Unfortunately, by remaining silent Emmanuelle was depriving herself of a possible means of finding Bee. She decided that, instead, she would question Ariane. But she did not see her short hair anywhere, or hear her bursts of laughter.

Had she found another victim to take into her little drawing room?

Marie-Anne spoke again of the elusive American girl. "I wanted to tell her good-by. Too bad for her. You'll have to do it for me."

"What! Is she leaving?"

"No, I am."

"You? You didn't tell me. Where are you going?"

"Oh, not far away, don't worry. I'm just going to spend a month at the seaside. My mother has rented a bungalow at Pattaya. You'll have to come and see me. It's not a long trip, even with the crowded roads—a hundred miles. You have to see those beaches, they're fantastic."

"I know, one of those blessed places where the sharks come and eat out of your hand. I'll never see you again."

"Where did you pick up that nonsense?"

"You're going to be bored there, all alone."

To her own surprise, Emmanuelle felt heavy-hearted. Unbearable as Marie-Anne was, she was going to miss her. But she did not want to let her see her sadness. She forced herself to laugh.

"I'm never bored anywhere," Marie-Anne said decisively. "I'll lie in the sun for hours, I'll go water-skiing. And I'm taking a suitcase full of books; I have work to do before school starts."

"That's true," Emmanuelle teased her, "I forgot you had to go back to kindergarten."

"Not everyone has your inborn knowledge."

"You won't have any friends with you at Pattaya?"

"No, thanks. I want to be left alone."

"That's very kind of you! I hope your mother will keep an eye on you and not let you run off with the fishermen's sons."

Marie-Anne's green eyes produced an enigmatic smile. "And you," she said, "what are you going to do without me? You'll fall back into your natural foolishness."

"No, I won't," Emmanuelle said banteringly, "you know very well that I'm going to give myself to Mario."

Marie-Anne instantly seemed to lose all taste for joking. "Yes, that's settled. You're not free any more."

"That's where you're wrong. I'll do whatever I want."

"All right, as long as you want Mario. You don't intend to back down now, do you?"

Marie-Anne seemed so disgusted that Emmanuelle was almost ashamed of herself. Yet she did not want to give in.

"He's not as irresistible as you claim. I find him a bit of a windbag. He makes phrases and listens to himself talk; he doesn't need another audience."

"Instead of being so fussy, you ought to consider yourself lucky that a man like Mario is interested in you. He's pretty hard to please, I can tell you that!"

"Oh? And he's interested in me? What an honor!"

"Exactly. I was glad to see you were making a fairly good impression on him. I can admit to you now that I wasn't very sure you would."

"Thanks. But would you mind telling me how you judged the effect I had on him? I had the feeling that he was paying attention only to himself."

"I know him a little better than you do; you'll at least admit that, won't you?"

"Of course. I naturally assume that you've long since granted him your favors. Maybe you should tell me some of the details of your experience with him, it will help me to be less self-conscious when it's time to make the sacrifice."

"You'd better stop being so silly if you don't want him to drop you," said Marie-Anne. "He can't stand stupidity." She abruptly became conciliatory. "But I know it's actually only a pose with you. Otherwise I wouldn't have introduced you to him . . . I'm sure you'll get along very well with him. You're going to be happy. And you'll be even more beautiful by the time I see you again. I want you to be always more and more beautiful."

Her jade eyes had become so soft that Emmanuelle was moved by them. "Marie-Anne," she murmured, "it's a pity you're going away."

Suddenly, as if intimidated, they exchanged a look of friendship. Then Marie-Anne renewed her demands, as though to return to an area less likely to require tender emotion. "I want you to promise me again that you'll behave intelligently with Mario."

"Oh, all right, if it makes you so happy."

For the first time since they had known each other, Marie-Anne brought her face close to Emmanuelle's and planted a quick kiss on her cheek. Emmanuelle put out her hands to hold her silky head against her, but she had already moved it away.

"I'll see you again soon, pussy cat! I'll call you tomorrow, before I leave. And you'll come to see me at the seaside."

"Yes," Emmanuelle said in a little voice.

"Now let's go back to the others."

They had moved away from the bulk of the crowd and they now mingled with it again. Emmanuelle passed from group to group without letting anyone latch onto her. She was looking for Ariane. It was Ariane who saw her first.

"Here you are again, Immaculate Virginia!" she cried. "I thought you were mortifying your flesh in some haven of penitence."

"Quite the contrary," Emmanuelle replied in the same tone. "A Prince of Darkness was comparing my laugh to the art of the strip tease."

"Who is that connoisseur?"

"I was only told his first name—Mario. But you must know who he is . . ."

"Oh, yes!" Ariane said gleefully. "With him, there's no danger that he'll try to put his gallant words into action! Your virtue would be more threatened if you were a handsome boy."

"You mean he's . . ."

"I'd be reluctant to mention it if he made any mystery of it himself. Hasn't he expounded his favorite theories to you yet? I see he hasn't really honored you with his confidence. He has fewer secrets with me. He's an exquisite man and I adore him."

"Maybe he hides some of his inclinations from me because I arouse others in him," retorted Emmanuelle, offended.

She was annoyed with Marie-Anne for having concealed that trait of her hero. It was unlikely that she was unaware of it, since she seemed to know everything.

"*Lasciate ogni speranza, voi ch'entrate!*" declaimed Ariane. "Your esthete is a man of principle. He won't let himself be turned away from his virtues and his ways."

"Oh, I've already depraved others, you know!" Emmanuelle boasted.

She was almost furious. Her aggressiveness delighted Ariane, who amused herself by stirring it up.

"I'm afraid you'll find that this one is incorruptible."

"We'll see."

"Bravo! The woman who converts Mario will deserve a golden Priapus." She lowered her voice. "But if I were in your place I wouldn't waste my time in the service of hopeless causes. I know a hundred men who are just as attractive as Mario, and would like nothing better than to do whatever you want them to. Shall I bring a few of them to you?"

"No. I like difficult victories."

"Well, then, good luck!" Ariane said mockingly. She looked at Emmanuelle as she had done at the club. "Have you had any pleasure these last few days?" she asked softly.

"Yes."

Ariane stared at her for a moment in silence. "With whom?"

"I'm not saying."

"But you did make love with someone, didn't you?"

"Yes."

Ariane gave her a friendly smile. "I've prepared something for you tonight, if you're willing."

"What is it?" Emmanuelle asked, curious in spite of herself.

"I'm not saying."

Emmanuelle sulked. Ariane relented: "A jumbo-sized jet pilot from London—a beauty!"

"Why don't you keep him for yourself?"

"And you?"

"You won't mind leaving me a few crumbs, will you?" Emmanuelle laughed, giving in to Ariane's lighthearted humor.

"Are you naked under your dress?" asked Ariane.

"Of course."

"Let's see."

This time, Emmanuelle was too perturbed to resist. They had gradually moved away from the other guests and were now separated from them by a screen. She took hold of the bottom of her skirt and lifted it.

"Good," said Ariane, with her eyes glued to Emmanuelle's black and ocher belly.

Emmanuelle felt those eyes fondling her sex, as though they were touching her, as though they were fingers or a tongue. She thrust herself forward to let their gaze lick her.

"Show more of yourself!" ordered Ariane. Emmanuelle tried to obey, but her dress was too tight to be raised any higher. "Take it off."

Emmanuelle nodded. She was eager to be naked. The tips of her breasts were demanding to be offered like the point of her sex. She pulled her shoulder straps down and pulled on the zipper under her armpit.

"Oh!" exclaimed Ariane. "Here come some intruders!"

The spell ceased to operate; Emmanuelle felt as if she had just come out of a dream. She closed her dress again and shook her hair. Ariane took her by the arm and led her farther away. A houseboy appeared, carrying a tray; they both drank a glass of champagne, in one gulp.

Ariane called back the servant and they exchanged their empty glasses for full ones. Emmanuelle was very thirsty. They no longer knew what to say to each other. They looked straight ahead, without seeing clearly, at those people who were chattering in high-pitched voices and bowing profusely to each other. It seemed to them that the temperature had risen. Maybe there was going to be a storm. Yes, that was it.

"Do you think there's going to be a storm?"

"I'm sure of it."

"How hot it is!"

Emmanuelle thought, "This dress is absurdly hot."

Someone motioned to Ariane and she seemed about to go away. Emmanuelle abruptly remembered what she wanted to ask her.

"Listen," she said, holding her back by a fold of her skirt, "do you know an American girl with red hair, dark red, almost copper-colored? She's the sister of a naval attaché. She—"

"Bee?" interrupted Ariane.

Emmanuelle's heart pounded. She would have found it normal that no one would know Bee, and, by a contradiction which revealed the disorder of her thoughts at that moment, even though she was specifically asking for information about her, she was annoyed to hear her nickname spoken by Ariane.

"Yes," she acknowledged. "Is she here this evening?"

"She was supposed to be, but I haven't seen her."

"Why shouldn't she have come, if she was invited?"

"I don't know."

Ariane suddenly seemed evasive, as if she wanted to change the subject. It was not like her and Emmanuelle persisted.

"What kind of a woman is she, in your opinion?"

"How did you get to know her?"

"I met her at a tea party, at Marie-Anne's house."

"Oh? It's not surprising. She's one of her friends."

"And you? Do you see her often?"

"Fairly often."

"What does she do in Bangkok?"

"The same thing you and I do. She arouses desire!"

"Why does her brother support her while she does nothing?"

"I don't think he supports her. She has a lot of money. She has no need of anyone."

These words resounded mournfully in Emmanuelle's heart. No need of anyone? She did not doubt it.

She did not know what else to ask. Without being able to explain it to herself, she was afraid to ask for Bee's address, as though this would have been an improper question.

"Well?" said Ariane.

Emmanuelle knew what was in her mind, but she pretended not to understand. Ariane became explicit: "Shall I take you to my visiting superman?"

"It's impossible . . . my husband . . ."

"He won't mind your going out with *me*!" said Ariane. But the temptation had passed and she was aware of it. "All right, then," she said, "I'll keep him all to myself."

Her good humor rang false. She, too, seemed to have lost her taste for dissipation. Emmanuelle felt that she would go home to sleep as soon as the reception was over.

"There's your Mario!" exclaimed Ariane. "He seems to be looking for someone. You, I'm sure! Don't make him languish." She pushed Emmanuelle by the arm.

But the Italian had already seen them and was walking toward them. Ariane left on the pretext that she was going to bring them something to drink; they did not see her again.

"Marie-Anne has told me a lot about you," said Mario.

This was not at all reassuring to Emmanuelle. "What can she have invented?"

"Enough to make me want to know you better. Will you have dinner with me some evening soon, so that we can talk together at leisure? There's no chance for us in this mob."

"Thank you, but we have a friend staying with us in our house now. It would be hard for me to . . ."

"Why? Let your husband take care of him for one evening. You have permission to go out alone, haven't you?"

"Of course," said Emmanuelle. She wondered what Jean would think. She added, with a certain malice, "But wouldn't you prefer me to bring my husband?"

"No," said Mario, without the slightest embarrassment. "I'm inviting you alone."

She had to give him credit for frankness, but she was still a little surprised—the style of his invitation was not in keeping with the reputation that Ariane had attributed to him. She wished she could find out exactly what the truth was.

"It's not very proper," she said playfully, "for a married woman to have dinner with a gentleman alone. Don't you agree?"

"Proper?" He articulated the word as though he had just heard it for the first time and found it, at the very least, difficult to pronounce. "Do you believe that you have to be proper? Is that one of your rules?"

"No, no!" she said defensively, in alarm. "Even so, it's more piquant for a woman to be warned in advance of the risks she's running."

"It all depends on what you mean by risk. What's your concept of the danger involved here?"

Emmanuelle felt as if she were again under cross-examination. If she referred to the duties of marriage, social standards, or morality, Mario's rejoinder was easy to foresee. On the other hand, she did not have enough courage or experience to admit outright what was on her mind. She could only say, rather pitifully, "I'm not afraid."

"That's all I ask of you," said Mario. "Will you come tomorrow night?"

"But I don't know where you live."

"Give me your address—I'll send a taxi for you." He smiled charmingly. "I don't have a car."

"I could come in mine."

"No, you'd get lost. The taxi will come for you at eight o'clock. Agreed?"

"Agreed."

She told him the section of the city, the street, and the number of her house.

He looked at her for a long time, inscrutably. Finally he announced his conclusion.

"You're beautiful," he said without grandiloquence.

"That's the least of it," she replied politely.

5
The Law

Come, my friends, 'tis not too late to seek a newer world.

— Alfred Lord Tennyson, "Ulysses"

Thou didst create night and I made the lamp,
Thou didst create clay and I made the cup,
Thou didst create the deserts, mountains, and forests,
I produced the orchards, gardens, and groves;
It is I who turn stone into a mirror,
And it is I who turn poison into an antidote.

— Mohammed Iqbal

Mario seated Emmanuelle on the sofa covered with red leather as supple as satin, between the Japanese lamps. A houseboy, wearing only a pair of tight, bright blue shorts that were open to expose his thighs, brought in a tray of glasses and knelt to set it down on the long, narrow table, covered with leather.

Mario's house was made of logs, overhanging a shimmering black canal. With only one floor, it looked like a hunting lodge from the outside. The luxury of its interior decor was all the more startling when one entered. One whole side of the drawing room opened onto the *khlong*. From where she was sitting, Emmanuelle could see boats made of bark, laden with sweet beverages, durians, coconuts, and lengths of bamboo filled with cooked rice gliding past the islets of vines and leaves that were drifting with the current. The man or the woman who stood straining over the single oar at the stern, swinging one foot, would glance placidly into the drawing room before melting away in the night. From the gable of a nearby temple, a little brass bell whose clappers, stirred by the wind, had the shape of a *bodhi* fig leaf, was tinkling in two notes, one high, the other low, as though wounded. In the distance, a gong was calling the Buddhist priests to sleep. A woman's voice began singing a shrill lullaby at a child's bedside.

"A friend will soon be here," said Mario.

His softened voice was in harmony with the shadows of Buddhist figures cast on the wall by the laconic light of the lamps. Emmanuelle felt a kind of physical apprehension, so much so that she gulped down half a glass of the strong cocktail that the houseboy had served her. But the shock of the alcohol was not enough to loosen the knot that had formed inside her. She rebuked herself for that shapeless fear, and tried to break the absurd enchantment.

"Do I know him?" she asked.

Only after she had spoken did she feel disappointment—so Mario didn't even care about being alone with her! She had thought he wanted to have her at his mercy, he had refused to let her bring her husband, and now he had invited someone else, a chaperon!

"No," he answered. "I met him only two days ago myself, at a social gathering. He's English. An engaging personality. And what amazing skin! The sun of this country has given him an even, toasted complexion . . . how shall I say? . . . a color that smells good. You'll like him."

Jealousy and humiliation clawed at Emmanuelle's heart. Mario spoke to her of that man with a greediness that made him pause before each word, apparently able to make his choice only after an inner debate. She imagined him with a tray in his hand, leaning over the display in a pastry shop. What doubt could she now have about his inclinations? Ariane had been right to warn her! At the same time, however, she had the disconcerting impression that his praise of his awaited guest's merits was not only for his own pleasure, but that it was also meant for her.

She was at a loss. If Mario wanted to take her, she had no objection. She was expecting it. That was why she had come, determined to go through with that misconduct to please Marie-Anne—or simply because the temptation was stronger than she was willing to admit, and the certainty of yielding to it gave her a pleasure as physical as the one she would soon feel in unfastening her dress herself, opening her legs, feeling a body whose touch and warmth had been unknown to her until now, entering her either all at once, in a delectable rape, or slowly, inch by inch, then withdrawing, leaving her waiting, open, dependent, supplicating, uncertain, and moist—what sweet suspense!—and returning, still as miraculously hard, swollen, and sharp as before, imperiously caressing the inside of her sex, voluptuously emptying itself to the last drop in her, not leaving her until she was seeded, until she was a field that had been dug, plowed, irrigated, appropriated . . . She bit her lips. She was ready. She loved that possession of her flesh. She desired it. But she wanted to be spared a complicated game— the idea of it tired her in advance. She should have been wary of the Italian spirit!

She was on the verge of saying to Mario, "You're right to take advantage of any opportunities that arise, but be content with the woman I am. Make love with me, then send me away to let me sleep beside my husband. When I'm gone, you can amuse yourself with your Englishman in any way you please." But she imagined how embarrassed she would be if he then looked at her with that expression of distant courtesy—of disdain—that she had already seen, and answered, "I'm afraid you have some mistaken ideas, my dear. I like you, of course, I like you a great deal, but . . ."

Mario's voice, with the very tone she had attributed to it in her thoughts, interrupted her imaginary scene.

"I want you to show as much of your legs as possible. Quentin will sit on that ottoman. Will you please turn in that direction, so he'll be facing your knees and can look into the shadows of your skirt?"

She felt bewildered. He put his hand on the bare skin of her shoulder, far enough forward to let his fingertips press the curve of her breast. He gently made her turn to the right while, with his other hand, he delicately took hold of her skirt and arranged it diagonally, so that it uncovered her legs unevenly, the left side up to the middle of the thigh, the right side almost to the groin.

"No, don't cross them," he said. "That's perfect. And whatever you do, don't move. Here he is." Mario's hand withdrew. She felt it slipping away from her as a wave leaves the beach.

He installed his guest on the ottoman, at the same time giving Emmanuelle a smile of encouragement, like a kindly examiner reassuring a frightened schoolgirl. But it was the Englishman who seemed almost intimidated. "He's not even looking at my legs," thought Emmanuelle, with less resentment than vindictive joy over the failure of Mario's machinations. It served him right! Quentin now seemed to her more an ally than an enemy. She admitted that he was rather pleasant to look at. It was true, she realized, he was quite handsome. And she had never seen anyone who looked less like a homosexual!

He was apparently incapable, unfortunately, of speaking a single word of French. "That seems to be my fate," Emmanuelle told herself ironically. "I'm doomed to meet only globetrotters who have no gift for foreign tongues." The ambiguity of the word "tongues" secretly amused her and goaded her to lascivious thoughts. She tried to imagine the sensations she would feel if Quentin's tongue were seeking hers, then descending to her belly. She pictured it penetrating her. Then she brought herself back to reality and made a heroic effort to use the few English phrases she had learned during her three weeks in Bangkok, but it did not take her far. Quentin, nevertheless, seemed delighted.

Mario obviously did not care to act as an interpreter. He mixed drinks and gave his servant explanations in a modulated language in which Emmanuelle did not recognize the inflections and sonorities of Thai, to which her ear was becoming accustomed. Finally he sat down in front of her, on the rug. He was three-quarters turned away from her, facing Quentin. They talked in English. Now and then Quentin looked at her and tried to include her in the conversation. After a time she decided that this had gone on long enough.

"I don't understand," she said.

Mario raised one eyebrow in surprise and replied, "It doesn't matter."

Then, before she had time to object to his impertinence, he leaped to his feet, sat down beside her, put his arm around her waist, made her lean back a little, and cried out to Quentin, with an enthusiasm and warmth that left her stupefied, *"Non è bella, caro?"*

He held her in that unbalanced position that forced her to raise her legs and—she realized, this time with a touch of amusement—uncover them more. He teased her lips with his fingers, then solemnly pulled down the top of her dress. First he bared one of her shoulders and her upper arm, then the tip of a breast. He contemplated it, rounding his lips. "She's really beautiful, isn't she?"

The Englishman nodded. Mario covered her breast. "Do you like her legs?" he asked in French. Quentin's only answer was to squint his eyes. Mario insisted: "They're *very* beautiful! And above all, they're pure organs of erotic pleasure, from hip to toe." He ran his fingertips along the lines of her golden thighs. "It's perfectly clear that their function is not to walk." He leaned over her. "I'd like you to give your legs to Quentin. Are you willing?"

She did not understand very well what he meant and her head was spinning a little. But she did not want to appear to back down, no matter what was asked of her. She decided to remain impassive. This seemed to satisfy him.

His hand raised her skirt again, but much higher. Because of its tightness, he had to lift her with his free arm to uncover the top of her thighs and lower belly entirely. That evening, for the first time since she had come to Bangkok, she was wearing stockings, in spite of the heat. In the diamond-shaped space marked off by her garter belt and the folds of her groin, her black panties, transparent as tulle, sedately held her silky curls in order.

"Come," said Mario, "take them."

She saw Quentin inch toward her. A hand caressed her ankles, then two. Then one again, while the other rose along one of her calves, then along the other, lingering in the hollows of her knees, at the beginnings of her thighs, finally moving around them and remaining there, as though awed by all the space that was offered beyond that last refuge of decency.

The other hand came to the assistance of the first and joined it to encircle her thighs, thin enough near her knees to fit almost entirely into the ring of fingers that was pressing them against each other.

Next, the two hands advanced together, first on the sides of her thighs, then along their tops, then beneath them, until they touched her buttocks. There they firmly pushed her legs apart so that they could rub their inner surfaces, so sensitive that she felt her lips swelling.

Mario was looking at her. But she did not see him. When she opened her eyes and tried to read in his what he was expecting of her, he merely smiled without letting her discern anything. Then, as much out of defiance as because she was avid for pleasure, she raised her skirt, already rolled up, still higher, took hold of her elastic panties, and pushed them down. The Englishman's hands instantly became bolder and more obliging; they helped her slip out of her panties and pulled them completely off.

Almost immediately Mario's voice, still deeper and softer than before, made Emmanuelle start. He was speaking in

English. After a few sentences he translated for her. "You mustn't grant everything to the same person," he said in the tone of someone teaching a difficult truth. "Quentin has had your legs; let him be satisfied with that, for the moment. Keep the rest of your body for others, on another occasion. One part of yourself to each man; play at first giving yourself bit by bit."

Emmanuelle did not dare to cry out, "But what do *you* want? Which part of me tempts you?" She wondered, with a touch of derision, whether the breast he had briefly touched was enough for him. For a second she hated him. But he stood up, cheerful and brisk, clapped his hands, and said, "Shall we have dinner now? Come, *cara*! I want you to taste some dishes that drive the body wild."

He picked her up from the sofa, with one arm under her shoulders and the other under her legs, which were still uncovered and seemed even longer from being thus suspended, sculpted in shadow and relief by the uneven light of the paper lamps. When he set her on her feet, her black skirt fell back down. She gracefully leaned to one side to smooth it out. She looked at a thin patch of dark nylon on the rug and did not know what to do. Mario deftly picked it up with his fingertips and pressed it to his lips.

"'Breaking with real things is nothing, but with memories! . . .'" he declaimed. "'The heart is broken by separation from dreams, so little reality is there in Man.'"

Then he slipped the perfumed panties into the breast pocket of his raw silk jacket. He took Emmanuelle, disconcerted, by the hand and led her to the little round table around which had been placed three high-backed old wooden chairs in quasi-medieval style.

She could not bring herself to look at Quentin. In spite of herself, however, she now enjoyed the strangeness of the experience and was beginning to forget her grievances against Mario. She even told herself, after thinking it over, that he had no doubt been right to prevent her from abandoning herself to that handsome young stranger, to whom she felt indifferent. After all, she was not going to open her body to every man who put his hand on her knee. It was already enough that she had behaved that way on the plane. With Mario, obviously, it was different . . . She agreed that there was nothing outrageous in a married woman's letting herself be shared by a husband and a lover. And now that Marie-Anne had put the idea into her head, she really wanted to have a lover. But only one! And she wanted that lover to be Mario . . . It suddenly occurred to her that, no matter what he claimed, he might have made her refuse herself to Quentin because he wanted to keep her for himself. This hypothesis brought back her good humor.

Yet she did not want to make things too easy for him. "I don't see how you can reconcile your 'love on the installment plan' with the esthetics you were professing last night," she remarked ironically. "If it's important to lavish and unmake oneself, why are you now exhorting me to be stingy with myself, to give myself in bits and pieces?"

"Then give yourself all at once! And when it's over?"

"Over?"

"When the woman who posed for the 'oval portrait' had given away her last color and emptied herself of her last breath, what art remained possible? *Finita la commédia*. When the last cry of pleasure has come from your lips, the work of art will be abolished. It will vanish like a dream, it will never have existed. Isn't the most imperious duty in this mortal world, the only duty, taking everything into account, to *make things last*? Unmake oneself? Certainly! But endlessly!"

"You and your disciple Marie-Anne should harmonize your teaching. She urges me to squander myself, you urge me to economize myself. And you both give the shortness of life as your reason!"

"I see you've totally misunderstood me, my dear! Little girls like Marie-Anne seem to have a talent for exposition that we elderly men lose with age."

"No, it's not that! You advocate continence . . ."

"That's the most unjust reproach I've ever heard!" Mario interrupted gaily. "But isn't your indignation liable to condemn us to abstinence?"

"How?"

"This soufflé is getting cold . . ."

Emmanuelle laughed a little sheepishly. It was too easy for Mario to elude embarrassing questions that way.

For a time they spoke of nothing but the food and wine. Quentin took only a modest part in the conversation, even though Mario flitted back and forth from one language to the other. Emmanuelle praised the refinement of the meal. She said that she usually attached little importance to what she ate, but that this evening she found that even she was sensitive to the quality of a roast.

"If gastronomy doesn't seem to you the most important thing in life, what does?" asked Mario.

She realized that the conversation was now allowed to rise to the heights it had failed to reach during the hors d'oeuvres. She reflected. What answer could she give, to remain within the tone of the house, yet without conceding too much to her host's despotism? After all, she told herself, the goal of that evening was clear—she had come there to be debauched, not to philosophize.

"Frequent orgasms," she said in a natural voice.

Mario seemed unappreciative, even impatient. "Yes, yes, of course," he said, "but should one simply have them? Is it the orgasm that matters most, or how one reaches it?"

"The orgasm—there's no doubt of it!" She did not really mean it; she was trying to provoke Mario. She seemed to have succeeded only in appalling him.

"Poor god," he sighed.

"Have you gotten religious?" she asked in surprise.

"It's an esthetic god I'm invoking. A god—Eros—whose laws you would do well to learn."

"Do you think I don't know how to serve him?" she bristled. "He's the god of love."

"No. He's the god of eroticism."

"Oh, that's what he's been made into!"

"Is a god ever anything else? You don't seem to have a very high opinion of eroticism."

"You're mistaken—I'm all for it."

"You are? And how do you understand it, exactly?"

"Well, eroticism is . . . how shall I say it? . . . It's the cult of the pleasure of the senses, freed of all morality."

"By no means. It's precisely the opposite."

"It's the cult of chastity?"

"It's not a cult, but the victory of reason over myth. It's not a movement of the senses, it's an exercise of the mind. It's not an excess of pleasure, but the pleasure of excess. It's not a license, but a rule. And it's a morality."

"Very pretty!" Emmanuelle applauded.

"I'm talking seriously. Eroticism is not a handbook of recipes for amusing yourself in society. It's a concept of human destiny, a gauge, a canon, a code, a ceremony, an art, a school. It's also a science—or rather the choice fruit, the last fruit, of science. Its laws are based on reason, not on credulity . . . on confidence, instead of fear . . . and on a taste for life, rather than on the mystique of death. Eroticism is not a product of decadence, but a progress. Because it helps to desanctify sex, it's an instrument of mental and social health. And I maintain that it's an element of spiritual elevation, because it presupposes character training and a renunciation of the passions of illusion in favor of the passions of lucidity."

"That sounds gay!" Emmanuelle said sarcastically. "Does it seem like a tempting picture to you? Isn't it more pleasant to have illusions?"

"The fury of possessing someone for oneself alone, or belonging to a single person; the will for power or servitude; the pleasure of making others suffer and die; fascination with, desire for, and love of suffering and death; an appetite for eternity—those are what I call passions of illusion. Do they tempt you?"

"Not really. But tell me what ought to tempt me."

"I'd like the supreme virtue to be the passion for beauty. It contains everything. What's beautiful is true, what's beautiful is justified, what's beautiful thwarts death. It's because of love of beauty that the world will ultimately refuse to sit in the theater of illusion where the masqueraders of politics and revelations act out their shadow play with regal slowness. The universe in motion will laugh at their immoble pretensions.

"But remember this: It's not in the finished work that beauty awaits you. It's not a success. Not the paradise promised to the loyal workman, or the serenity of twilight after the piety of toil. It's a creative blasphemy that's never silent, a question that nothing satisfies, a forward march that never wearies. It's what challenges us in the black suicidal gifts of our accidental matter. It identifies itself with the heroism of our destiny.

"Beauty was not given to Man by a god. Man invented it. Beauty is Man's seditious hope against the given order, the virtue born of his feeling of pride and strangeness in a universe from which he has banished angels and devils. It's the promised victory over grass and rain, the sirens' flight above the hideousness of the ocean. For beauty is the wing of the world; without it, the mind would be grounded. That's why I say that eroticism, that triumph of the dream over nature, is the lofty refuge of the spirit of poetry, because it denies the impossible. It is Man who can do *anything*."

"I don't have a very clear idea of that power," objected Emmanuelle.

"The sex act between women is a biological absurdity, it's impossible. Eroticism immediately makes a reality of that invention of the dream. Sodomy is a defiance of nature; eroticism commits sodomy. Intercourse by five people at once is not *natural*; eroticism imagines it, orders it, and carries it out. And each of its victories is *beautiful*. It's true that eroticism doesn't need these exceptional arrangements in order to flourish; it demands only youth and freedom of the mind, love of truth, and a purity that owes nothing to custom and convention. Eroticism is a passion of courage."

"Your eroticism sounds like a kind of asceticism! Is it really worth going to all that trouble?"

"It's worth a thousand times more! If only for the pleasure of flouting our monsters. To begin with, the most hideous of all—stupidity and cowardice, those two Hydras so dear to men! To men who have never confessed themselves so well as in Hobbes' cry, truer each morning after three centuries: 'The single passion of my life will have been fear!' Fear of being different. Fear of thinking. Fear of being happy. All those fears that are antipoetry and have become the values of the world—conformity, respect for taboos and rites, hatred of imagination, refusal of novelty, masochism, malevolence, envy, pettiness, hypocrisy, lying, cruelty, shame. In a word, evil! The true enemy of eroticism is the spirit of evil."

"And to think that I believed some people called eroticism what others simply called vice!" Emmanuelle mused ironically.

"Vice, you say? What do you mean by that word? 'Vice' means 'defect.' Eroticism, like all the other works of Man, is not free of defects, errors, and relapses. If that's the case, then let's say that vice is the price of eroticism, its shadow, its waste matter. But there's one thing that cannot exist—shameful eroticism. The qualities required for the birth of the erotic act—logic and firmness of mind above all, imagination, humor, and daring, to say nothing of power of conviction, organizational ability, good taste, esthetic intuition, and a sense of grandeur, without which all its attempts fail—must necessarily make it something proud, generous, and triumphant."

"Is that why you present it as a morality?"

"No, it's because of much more than that. Eroticism demands above all a systematic mind. Its partisans can only be men of principle, makers of theories—no joyous carousers or circus strongmen announcing the number of shots they've fired, after drinking, with little chambermaids who like to dance."

"In short, eroticism is the opposite of making love?"

"That's going too far. But it's true that making love is not necessarily an act of eroticism. There's no eroticism where there's sexual pleasure that springs from impulse, habit, or duty; where there's a pure and simple response to a biological instinct, a physical purpose rather than an esthetic one, a pursuit of the pleasure of the senses rather than the pleasure of the mind, love of oneself or another rather than love of beauty. In other words, there's no eroticism where there's *nature*. Eroticism, like all morality, is an effort by Man to oppose nature, surmount it, surpass it. You know very well that Man is Man only to the extent that he has made himself a *denatured* animal, and that he becomes more human only insofar as he separates himself more from nature. Eroticism, the most human talent of men, is not the opposite of love, it's the opposite of nature."

"Like art?"

"Bravo! Morality and art are one. I commend you for speaking of art as antinatural. Haven't I already told you that beauty was found only in the defeat of nature? In every age, the makers of shadows on the wall of our lives have tried to convince men, usually by kicking them, that they can be cured of the fatigue of machines and architecture only by a 'return to nature.' What a disgusting panic, what an abominable degradation of intelligence! A return to the vermin of humus—is that the whole future deserved by the inventors of mathematics and ballerina tights? If this species is eager to end, then let it go out in a blaze of glory, in a spray of atoms. It would be better to have an empty spot among the heavenly bodies and the memory of a final song of pride than a planet populated by one more race of monkeys. I hate nature!" He abruptly put his hand down on hers and squeezed it almost hard enough to make her cry out.

His voice became strangely beautiful "I was flying over the Gulf of Corinth, on my way to the country whose night we're now sharing. To my right, the peaks of the Peloponnesus were covered with snow. To my left, the golden beaches of Attica were warming the sea. A newspaper that was brought to me turned me away from that spectacle for a moment, but not to betray it, because it proclaimed the most beautiful poem that man has ever written—a poem whose ancient roots plunged into the very land that was offering me its adorable lips, half-opened above the lustrous waves and blistered by sunlight, the same dawn as the morning of the Odyssey and, after so many miraculous years, swollen with the same desire of the sirens, still as headstrong and mad for knowledge, wary and wise . . . Here is that poem: 'On January 3, at 3:57 A.M., a white star will appear at the center of the triangle formed by the stars Alpha of Boötes, Alpha of Libra, and Alpha of Virgo.'

"That star has now appeared, a minute steel pebble thrown by Man, as though from a sling, at the face of the universe. And the new age that has begun is ours forever. From now on, our earth and the flesh of our race may perish, but one more star, a star made by our hand, stamped with our mark and speaking words of our language, will be eternally turning, ruining by its song the cold majesty of infinite space. O you, you Alpha stars, whose vigil has crossed out our remorseless conquest, our taste for life stretches its bare legs on your beaches of fire!"

Mario closed his eyes and did not begin speaking again until several minutes had gone by. His voice had regained its disdainful slowness.

"Art, you said? The most perfect artistic creation is that which moves farthest from the image of God. Ah, how unimportant is what God has created, compared with the work of men! How beautiful our planet is, now that we've filled in its hollows, now that we've erected our glass palaces on it, and made its ether vibrate at the frequency of our cantatas! How beautiful it is, drawn from God's night by Man's light! How beautiful it is, liberated from God's underbrush and snakes by the growth of Man's cities! How beautiful it is, trimmed of its landscapes and adorned with the iron creatures of its Calders, the squares of gold, blood, and sky, and the lines of its Mondrians! The kingdom of Man on earth and in the skies is too beautiful for us to concern ourselves any longer with the kingdom of God!" He looked at Emmanuelle as though he saw in her face those forms and fires of the earth he loved.

"Wasn't it by means of art that the Quaternary hominid separated himself from the wild animal and became Man? He is the only living creature that will leave more in the universe than he found. But already the art of colors, curves, and sounds is no longer sufficient to satisfy his creative passion. He wants to fashion his own flesh and his own thought in the image of his genius, as he once drew Apsaras and Corae from his dream. The art of this age can no longer be an art of cold stone, bronze, or paint. It can only be an art of living bodies, it can only 'live from life.' The only art that fits spaceman, the only one capable of taking him farther than the stars—as figures drawn with ocher and soot opened the walls of the cave onto the future—is eroticism.

"Tell me," he continued, "is there any art more poignant than the art that takes the human body and, from that work of nature, makes its own denatured work? It's easy for a skilled craftsman to draw from marble or the rhythm of lines an object whose paternity he hasn't had to wrest from the universe. But to work with Man! To seize him in one's hands, not like a lump of clay, not in order to feel his texture and his contours, or approve of him, or love him, or enjoy him, but precisely in order to contest his form and content, remove him from the idiotic groping of the cell, alter his very composition, extract his abject nature from him, as one delivers a laboratory animal from the heredity that made it a slug or a rodent. To remake Man! To save him from matter, in order to make him free to give himself his own laws, laws that no longer lump him together with the meteor and the molecule, laws that liberate him from the decline of energy and from gravity. That, truly, is more than art . . . it's the reason for being of the mind itself."

He stood up and walked to the opening that overlooked the *khlong*. "Look!" he said. "The gulf is not between animate and inanimate; it's between what's conscious and the rest of the world. That lizard and that dog aren't different from trees and seaweed, which aren't different from water and stone. But look at those boatmen rowing and dreaming, decked out in their rags, with their persistence, their clenched fingers, their short hair . . . There's Man! Ah, it takes a frenzied love of men to be able to hate nature well. Men, men, how I love you! You'll go so far!"

"For you, then," Emmanuelle asked almost timidly, "the only possible love is unnatural love?" She accompanied her question with an affectionate laugh intended to show him that she was not trying to offend him. But there was no risk of that. As usual, he demolished the idea with words.

"That's a truism. And a redundancy. Love is always unnatural. It's the absolute antinature. It's the crime, the insurrection par excellence against the order of the universe, the false note in the music of the spheres. It's Man escaping from the Garden of Eden with a burst of laughter. It's the failure of God's plans."

"And you call that moral!" Emmanuelle joked.

"Morality is what makes Man Man! Not what makes him an alienated object, a captive, a slave, a eunuch, a penitent, or a buffoon. Love wasn't invented to debase him, subjugate him, or make him grimace. It's not the poor man's cinema or the restless soul's tranquilizer; it's not a diversion, or a game, or a drug, or a toy. Love, the art of carnal love, is Man's reality, the only firm ground, the only real homeland. 'Everything that is not love takes place for me in another world, the world of phantoms. Everything that is not love takes place for me in a dream, and in a hideous dream . . . I do not become a man again until arms enfold me!' That penetrating cry of Don Juan's has been heard and understood by so many others, no matter how different the forms of their genius. 'Do you think love is a pastime? Gyrlimo, it's a task, and the hardest of all.'"

"I don't agree," said Emmanuelle. "I prefer to think of love as a pleasure rather than as a duty."

"The morality of eroticism is that pleasure makes morality."

"I feel that a moral pleasure loses a good part of its appeal."

"Why?" he asked with surprise. "I don't understand. Is it because you identify moral principles with deprivation and coercion? But what if a principle deprives you of depriving yourself? What if it obliges you to take advantage of life? The idea of morality repels you because you confuse it with the idea of sexual prohibition. To you, moral conduct means 'Thou shalt not be impure in body or mind; thou shalt desire the act of the flesh only in marriage.' Don't let that hoax discredit the honorable word 'morality' in your eyes. Don't use a ludicrous imposture, long since exposed, as a pretext for condemning both good and evil, or—and this is even more serious—saying that good and evil don't exist!

"You surely realize that it was through fraud that sexual taboos gained admission into the kingdom of morality and finally subjugated it to their unjust law. They had no place in it by divine right. In fact, their nature and purpose are totally immoral, since they originally sprang from an eminently pragmatic motive—to assure the landholder of the ownership of children, who were instruments of production and outer signs of wealth, like flint pickaxes and pottery."

He leaped up and walked to a shelf laden with books, in the deep red semidarkness, and returned holding a volume.

"I don't choose or appeal to my texts improperly," he said. "I limit myself to the most irrefutable of dogmas: the Commandments brought back from Mount Sinai by Moses. And in the seventeenth verse of the twentieth chapter of Exodus I read, carved in stone, the following: 'Thou shalt not covet thy neighbor's house, thou shalt not covet thy neighbor's wife, nor his manservant, nor his maidservant, nor his ox, nor his ass, nor any thing that is thy neighbor's.' There, it's directly and unambiguously stated. Woman, know the place that the Eternal has assigned to you—between the barn and the livestock, with the rest of the laborers. And not in the first rank, either. Wife, you come after brick and thatch. Maidservant, you have less value than a farmhand, and just a little more than a horned animal or a donkey." He closed his Bible and put his right hand on it, pastorally.

"It is said that the Middle Ages invented love. The fact is that the Middle Ages nearly succeeded in making us disgusted with it! In giving us the poisoned gift of his 'morality,' the feudal cleric thought he was cutting off our desire for sexual pleasure forever. Look at what's left of his plots and contrivances! The chastity belts of good and evil that the lords of the earth fastened onto their wives and their she-asses are now falling in rusty fragments from the battlements and parapets that witnessed their birth. Let's do them the honor of putting them in a museum. But let's first note that their end is eminently moral—though their birth was not! And let's marvel at the fact that real morality is what subsists after the work of time has dealt with false morality as it deserves."

Emmanuelle was thoughtful. She agreed with Mario's view of the contingent value of the imperatives of traditional morality, but, precisely because of that, it seemed senseless to waste time building a new morality on the ruins of the old one. Couldn't she simply make love as she pleased, freely, without racking her brain to draw up a new code and announcing it from the housetops? Was it really necessary to give herself formed laws? There was no morality anywhere, not even an "erotic" one, she thought, that could be better than no morality at all.

"You can't triumph over bad laws by anarchy," Mario retorted when she had expressed these doubts to him. "The idea is not to return to the jungle, but to recognize that some of Man's powers, which society now represses and condemns to atrophy, are just, and that they give our species the means of happiness. The new law, the good one, simply proclaims that it's beautiful and good to make love well and freely; that virginity is not a virtue, two lovers not the limit, or marriage a prison; that the art of erotic pleasure is what matters and that we must constantly offer ourselves, give ourselves, unite our bodies with more and more bodies, and count all time spent out of their arms as wasted." He raised his finger. "If you hear me add other laws to this great one, remember that they're nothing more than secondary regulations whose purpose is to help in observing the principle I've just set forth, by rejecting timidity of the soul and weariness of the flesh."

"But," said Emmanuelle, "if the taboos of bourgeois morality have an economic origin, there will have to be a real revolution before your erotic morality can be put into effect."

"It requires something much more important and much more radical than a revolution—a mutation like the mutation by which the fish that was tired of the sea, and was one day to be called Emmanuelle, wanted to find out if its new liking for land would make it grow legs, and began breathing by raising its future breasts."

She smiled at the image. "So erotic Man will be a new animal?"

"He'll be more than Man, and yet he'll still be Man. Simply more adult, further advanced on the scale of evolution. The day is coming when, just as surely as artistic values separated men from beasts, the values of eroticism will separate the proud man from the ashamed man who huddles in the dens of present society, hiding his nakedness and chastising his sex. Poor, human, rough drafts that we are, sketches still coated with the mud of the Pleistocene swamps! In love with our inhibitions and our crude sufferings, struggling with all our blindness and all our evangelical brute strength against the currents of hope that try to draw us out of childhood!"

"But what makes you think that those currents will win out, that your morality will eventually triumph over the morality that's protected by religious custom and law? What if the opposite were to happen?"

"It won't! I won't believe it! Because I can't believe that Man has come from so far and so low only to stop here and suddenly give up moving forward, being something else. He'll go on! Groping his way, yes, and shuddering, but without ever turning back, making himself more and more different from the other species. If we're already less stupid than the coelacanth, it means that some day the gap will be even greater."

He gave her a few moments to reflect.

"What we're capable of is trying to add to intelligence, and to do the impossible to be happy. I've been given no promise that I'll ever find the unexplored shore that I can only call happiness, yet Eluard was right to proclaim, 'It's not true that it takes everything to make a world. It takes happiness, and nothing else.' But what courage we need to attain it! The human animal has already shown great courage from childhood, in tearing himself away from the nursery of his gods. And he still shows it today in choosing not to wait in solitary contemplation for the kingdom where the meek and humble in heart will be rewarded, but rather to join the people of the streets in running the risk of life and death without paradise."

"And the risk of being mistaken," Emmanuelle pointed out, "of deluding himself about his nature. And the risk of what he thinks are his own ideas about his power and his importance."

He stared at her with sudden suspicion. "Are you on the side of those for whom Man's adventure has no meaning? Do you maintain that our species is doomed to failure, a failure in proportion to its naïveté? Do you think that we're the playthings of our own language, and that our downfall is inscribed on sovereign tablets? Is it your disdainful conviction that we've been invented, like the dodo bird, for the sole purpose of becoming extinct, and that that's all we're good for? Perhaps you even feel that Man's extinction will be the best thing that can happen to the world he's disrupted, and you're waiting for it, from the heights of your cold, inhuman knowledge, with the masochistic impartiality that's now in fashion?"

"No, I don't think that way," said Emmanuelle. "But you must admit that your own confidence is also a faith. A kind of religion."

"That's not true. If I'm sure of Man, it's because I see him at work. His progress, which is mine, consists in believing less and less and seeing better and better. Gods are born only behind closed eyelids."

"Maybe you look only at Einsteins, and not enough at criminals. Otherwise, you'd sometimes be afraid."

"Not being Einstein isn't a crime, but it's certainly a defect. And I have no right to complain that men are killing me if I myself have been unable to cure them of death. I may die, but I'll know that it's my weakness and not my honor."

"You know very well that no one will ever find a remedy for death."

"I know that it's the mind that dies when our mythologies, like tumors of the flesh, replace the happy cells in it. Disorder reigns where the chance of our reality existed. We die only of ignorance and ugliness. Death is nothing but the stupor of knowledge. The infinite expansion of intelligence is asymptotic to death. Therefore our future is infinite. We're no longer Doctor Eternal's patients; our patience is exhausted! We'll forget our mortal mornings as those who are cured forget their disease. We'll find our world in some haven of space-time; it will be our love and our reason. And we'll spend the long vigils of our illusion-less lives listening to the din of the quasars. We'll be happy . . ." He fell silent.

Emmanuelle let sufficient time go by, then, with a certain caution in her voice, brought him back to the subject. "And eroticism is capable of helping in the discovery of that new world?"

"More than that! It's identical with it, it's progress itself."

"Aren't you exaggerating?"

"Try to understand! I've told you the goal is not to reform society, or even to conceive a new one, to build a republic of lechery! The goal is biological progress, a transformation, a click that will be heard some morning in the future in a man's brain. A flash, and there it is! He thinks differently, he's another being. He's taken a step. The ignorance, terror, and servitude of his former race no longer concern him. He no longer even understands what they mean. It matters little whether or how he makes love. What's new is that he does it with a free mind. Good is what gives him pleasure, evil is what causes him suffering. It's as simple as that. There's his good and his evil. There's his morality. And his good is what's beautiful, what tempts him, what gives him an erection. His evil is what's ugly, what bores, limits, or frustrates him. Mystic trances and the delights and poisons of anxiety will no longer touch him. He'll no longer need hallucinogenic mushrooms, philosophers, or hermitages to cure himself of despair. His liking for himself and his fellow human beings will be enough for him. Doesn't that man seem to you a more advanced animal than the haircloth wearer? Hasn't he made progress?"

"Yes, I agree. But it's an individual progress, it has consequences only for him. Just now you were talking about progress as though it concerned the human race."

"It does. It's not by masses, by whole societies, that species evolve. Mutations have always occurred in a small number, one of those unloved minorities, with heads erect and eyes open, with which the great, flabby herds refused to share their pastures. But when one of those mutant branches grows out of the human tree, the whole world is changed. If tomorrow a man appears for whom the words 'immodesty,' 'adultery,' and 'incest' are meaningless, a man who couldn't understand them even if he tried, then our virtues will be relegated to museum displays, along with the teeth of the pterodactyl and the bony plates of the stegosaurus."

"But since that man hasn't appeared yet, the erotic age is only a vision of the future. You and I are unlucky—we were born too soon!"

"Who can say? The laws of evolution are still largely hidden from us. It may not be useless to try to bring ourselves into the world. Perhaps we haven't yet been born."

"What can we do to be born?" cried Emmanuelle.

"We can act as if we were the masters of life. Act as if we were alive! What may give us light is the practice of eroticism as the rule of life. And if enough of us adopt the scale of erotic values as the only scale, without reserve, in all clarity, ostentatiously, it's not we alone who will be enlightened—luck may smile on our species once again. Think of the first quadruped who decided once and for all that he was going to walk on his hind legs, without worrying about whether or not the rest of the animal kingdom would rather go on sniffing dung. Our determination to change for a prouder posture may be the decisive step, the necessary and sufficient condition for passing from the age of fear to the age of reason." He sighed.

"Ah, of course we'd prefer to be born a million years from now! Let's at least do our best to bring that age of reason closer to us. Nothing deserves to be done, said, or written today if it doesn't help us to 'pass.' We must watch our words and our simplest acts. We mustn't say or do anything that might confirm men in the idiotic conviction that they've already found what they came to seek. Nothing that might retard their puberty still longer. For my part, I know my duty—to repeat to them ceaselessly that the body is just, that its powers are infinite, that the sweetness of living is also life's reason for being."

* * *

The sound of Quentin's voice made Emmanuelle start—she had forgotten his presence. She listened to him talking to Mario with unexpected warmth and loquacity. Mario seemed greatly interested. Now and then he uttered exclamations of pleasure. Finally, he translated for Emmanuelle, who realized that the Englishman must have followed the main drift of their conversation more easily than she would have thought.

"What Quentin has told me makes all hopes possible. It seems that the 'mutant branch'—or at least a bud of that branch—exists already and, even better, has existed for a thousand years! For several months, Quentin was the guest of a tribe in India, the Muria. The 'civilized' Hindus call them 'primitive,' but there's every reason to believe that they're actually a vanguard of intelligence. Their society is constructed entirely around a sexual morality that is the exact opposite of ours . . . a morality that's not prohibitive, but formative. The cornerstone of their system of education is a community dormitory that children of both sexes enter at a very early age, to serve their apprenticeship in the art of love. This institution is called the '*Gothul.*' There, long before puberty, the little girls are initiated into physical love by the big boys, and the little boys by the big girls. And by no means in an instinctive or bestial way—the erotic techniques that are inculcated in them have, it seems, after ten centuries of practice, attained a level of incomparable refinement. This course of instruction, which all children are required to follow for several years, also serves to develop them artistically, because they spend their spare time—when they're not making love—decorating the walls of their dormitory. Their drawings, paintings, and sculptures are always erotically inspired. Quentin tells me they're so well done that no one can visit such a gallery without immediately being filled with very strong feelings. And when you've seen eleven-year-old boys and girls imitating the most daring figures in that museum of love without hiding or showing embarrassment, with the doors wide open, before their parents' proud gaze, executing living tableaus that in Europe would take them straight to a reform school, it quickly occurs to you that the Muria are not living a thousand years behind our time, but a thousand years in advance."

When Mario stopped speaking, Quentin gave him more details, which were in turn translated for Emmanuelle.

"The most remarkable part of it is that this sexual 'laboratory instruction,' which all the children of the tribe participate in, is the result of a system, a set of rigorous and elaborate rules, and not of moral laxity, or some sort of congenital moral blindness. It's not a matter of license, it's a matter of ethics. The community discipline of the *Gothul* is very strict; the older children are responsible for the younger ones. The 'law' rigorously forbids any lasting attachment between boys and girls. No one has the right to say that a certain girl is *his,* and a boy is punished if he spends more than three straight nights with any one girl. Everything is organized to prevent intense attachments that drag on indefinitely, and to eliminate jealousy. 'Everyone belongs to everyone.' If a boy shows an instinct of ownership and exclusiveness toward a girl, if his face goes to pieces when he sees her having intercourse with another boy, the community brings him back to the right path by helping him to overcome his nature. He must make active efforts to have the girl he loves possessed by all the other boys, he must guide their members into her with his own hand, until he has learned not only to suffer from it, but to wish it and be glad of it. With the Muria, the great crime is not theft or murder, *which do not exist,* but jealousy. Thus, by the time the girls and boys come to marriage, they're not only rich with a sexual knowledge and skill that's unique in the world, they also belong to another age of the earth—the resentments, grievances, and despairs of our civilization are foreign to them. They're on the side of happiness."*

Emmanuelle seemed impressed, yet she protested. "Mario, a morality of that kind can't be developed within a people by an effort of awareness and reflection. I'm sure the Muria have always had it. It must be an inborn grace. Let me remind you that a little while ago you put the gift of eroticism on the same level as the gift of poetry. That means it can't be acquired by will or intelligence. If it wasn't given to you by nature when you were born, you'll never get it, no matter how hard you try."

"What a common illusion that is! Must I tell you again that there's no other poetry in nature than what has been

---

* See Verrier Elwin's *The Muria and Their Ghotul* (Bombay: Oxford University Press, 1947).

put there by Man? No other harmony, no other beauty. And although Man does everything, nothing comes to him, including poetry and genius, until the age of reason. The example of the Muria simply shows that one can reach that age when one is more or less young. No man is born a poet. No people is born a chosen people. No one is born anything. One must learn. Our way of becoming men, of mutating into men, is to reject our ignorance and our myths, like a hermit crab casting off its old shell, and don truth like a new garment. Thus we can be indefinitely born and reborn. With each 'abrupt mutation,' we'll be more human and we'll remake our world to suit our pleasure better. 'Learning' is learning to enjoy. Ovid already said it, as you'll recall: '*Ignoti nulla cupido!*'"

Emmanuelle did not recall. Without troubling to enlighten her, Mario went on. "And what don't we have to learn! Art, morality, science—the beautiful, the good, the true; in short, everything, because nothing else exists, the time of the sacred is over. Fortunately, to make our task easier, that everything has produced a child of its own—Eros. Therefore erotic reflection, experience, and insight are all we need in order to attain poetry, morality, and knowledge, since these are actually only diverse reflections of a single lesson: the *man lesson,* in the sense that one speaks of an object lesson."

"Your demonstration is becoming more and more abstract, Mario! Why don't you give me some examples of what can be done?"

"Imagining, seeing, and if necessary, provoking those unexpected attitudes, encounters, and associations without which there can be no poetic situation—there, for example, is one of the sources of eroticism."

"You say 'unexpected'—does that mean you can't find pleasure in something you expect? Can't anything be erotic without being disconcerting?"

"It must at the very least be something that breaks with habit. A pleasure ceases to have an artistic quality if it's a usual pleasure. Only the nonbanal, the exceptional, the unfamiliar have value. Nothing can be truly erotic that isn't *unusual*."

"But then, when erotic morality has become established, won't eroticism lose its attractiveness? Can it be that, for the Muria, making love is no more amusing than making bread?"

"That's not the impression I got from what Quentin told me. Instead, it seems that, being experts in the art of love from childhood, they place nothing above sexual games all through their lives. They're known in India as fervent advocates of physical love. But I grant you that their experience isn't necessarily valid for us, since our minds are still marked, crippled forever, perhaps, by traditions of sexual hypocrisy that are stronger than the obvious conclusions of reason. We must hope, of course, that nature will make a leap for us. But in any case, let's not flatter ourselves that we're capable of guessing and usefully describing in advance what the psychology of our descendants, the mutants, will be. We who haven't yet 'taken the step' must concern ourselves only with our own adventure. And we must recognize that, for the prisoners that we are, the liberating miracle of erotic emotion usually occurs only when there's a defiance of accepted behavior. So it's true, and it's our revenge, that the present survival of false moral rules—or simply of social conventions—gives us, who refuse them, the power to shock. The woman whose husband impregnates her in her bed, before sleep, is not erotic. The erotic woman is the one who, at snack time, calls her son and tells him to prepare a sperm sandwich for his little sister. That's erotic because that menu hasn't yet become commonplace. When the bourgeoisie has adopted it, something else will have to be found."

"So I was right in saying that if eroticism needs the extraordinary, the unfamiliar, its very progress puts it in danger. One fine day it will have used up all its possibilities."

"You can even say without risk, my dear, that for a long time no one has invented anything. Nevertheless, your fears are vain, because eroticism isn't a heritage, it's a personal adventure. Eroticism will keep its value as an individual conquest even when Mankind has been freed of sexual taboos. Has the public nature of the laws of versification ever kept the poet from rediscovering the secret of poetry on his own?"

Emmanuelle nodded in agreement.

"What justifies the artist's enterprise," Mario continued, "is not innovating for history, but for himself. Unlike the inventions of science, the inventions of art lose nothing from having been already made! What does it matter if a horse has already been drawn by the Chinese or the cavemen of Lascaux? The first time my fingers extract a horse from the tenderness of my vision, he carries me on his four legs as far as the universe interests me. That is, let me say in passing, as long as he and I can be seen together, as long as I can show him off. We need society to look at us. There can be no happy art without a spectator."

He scrutinized Emmanuelle, awaiting a reaction. She showed none.

"The children of the Muria," he went on, "make love in front of their companions, or a passing visitor. If they were alone together in a bedroom, the chances are that they would eventually become bored. You're afraid that habit dulls pleasure. You're right. But don't we have the gaze of others to open up new horizons for us?" His voice took on a certain affectation. "At this point we come to a second law of eroticism: that it needs *asymmetry*."

"What do you mean? And besides, what was the first law?"

"That of the *unusual*. But both of them, as I've told you, are only 'little laws.' The great law, the only necessary and sufficient one, you'll remember, is supremely simple . . ."

"That all time spent doing anything but taking pleasure 'artfully,' always in different arms, is wasted. Is that it?"

"More or less, although I don't like the expression 'always in different arms.' It seems to imply that you must reject your old partners as soon as you acquire new ones. That would be the worst mistake! The quality of your pleasure will arise from increasing the number of your partners, rather than making them replace one another. Eros hides his secrets from fickle hearts! What good does it do to give yourself if it's only to take yourself back? The world will not become greater for you."

Emmanuelle frowned and bit her thumb, the very image of concentration, trying to think of how she could improve her argument. This stylistic exercise delighted her and Mario was aware of it.

"Furthermore," he said, "although I know how dear the idea is to you, I personally wouldn't put the main stress on *pleasure,* but, as I've already explained, on *art.* Will you forgive me?"

"All right, then," she said in a conciliatory tone, "instead of 'taking pleasure artfully,' let's say 'the art of pleasure.' Would you be satisfied with this: 'All time spent on anything but the art of pleasure, in increasingly numerous arms, is wasted'?"

"Very good!" approved Mario. "You have a sense of formulation, a talent for synthesis. You realize, of course, that in your statement the word 'arms' mustn't be given a narrow meaning. Needless to say, it covers a very broad range of erotic relations, from your own arms to anything besides your partner's arms— his eyes, his ears, even if they're invisible, behind a door, or at the end of a telephone wire—his letters, even his secret image in the depths of your heart. And, naturally, arms don't have any gender any more than they have number . . . But let's not digress into grammar."

"And perhaps 'the art of love' would be more graceful than 'the art of pleasure.'"

"More graceful, no doubt, but less precise. Besides, 'love' is ambiguous. Too limited, also; it takes at least two to love, while one can have pleasure alone."

"Of course."

"In fact, one *must* take pleasure alone. The kingdom of eroticism will always be closed to anyone who can't open its gates to his solitude." He looked at her sternly. "You do know how to take pleasure with yourself, don't you?"

She nodded.

"And do you like it?"

"Yes, very much."

"Do you do it often?"

"Very often."

She felt no shame in proclaiming it; quite the contrary. In this, too, Jean had encouraged her. And it would no more have occurred to her to conceal herself from him when she masturbated than when she took a bath; in fact, finding it perfectly understandable that he should like to look at her, she always tried to do both at times when he could see her. It seemed to her a conjugal duty at least as important as the others, and she knew he felt the same and appreciated her consideration.

"Then it will be easy for you to understand what the law of asymmetry means," said Mario. "It derives from the fact that there can be no progress without a certain imbalance at the beginning. Life and eroticism abhor equilibrium. Moreover the art of eroticism requires asymmetry to secure the presence of a public. For example, the number of those who make love must be odd."

"Oh?" said Emmanuelle, more amused than shocked.

"There's no doubt of it. One, for example, is an odd number—the masturbator is both actor and spectator. That's why masturbation is eminently erotic, a work of art. The only love that can be allowed to be exclusive.

> *"'A virgin entwined with herself,*
> *Jealous . . . But of whom, jealous and threatened?'"*

Mario seemed to be daydreaming for a moment. Then he continued: "Adultery is also erotic. The triangle redeems the banality of the pair. No eroticism is possible for a couple without the addition of a third party. It's true that the third party is nearly always there! If not in person, at least in the mind of one of the partners. While making love, haven't you ever been visited by the image of someone other than the person whose caresses you're savoring? Isn't your husband's hard flesh made softer when, at the same time, your closed eyelids give you in imagination to one of his friends, the husband of one of your friends, a man you passed in the street, a screen hero, your childhood lover? Answer. Do you like that? Do you do it?"

Emmanuelle nodded, with no more hesitation than she had shown a short time earlier. Merely recalling all the times when she had known the embraces of other men that way, while she was in Jean's arms, aroused such strong physical excitement in her that she thought Mario must be able to see it. The night before, it was to him that she had thus given herself . . . As she had given herself to Christopher on the night of his arrival. To Ariane's friends, without even knowing them. To Jean's brother, since she had known him. And so often, during the past weeks, to the strangers in the plane—especially the Greek god. All these faces came back to her with such warmth that she felt faint and did not dare to make the slightest gesture, for fear of being unable to restrain her hand.

"You won't fail to notice," Mario said with a mocking smile, "that the erotic seal would be missing if both partners behaved in the same manner—when one of them slips away, the other must be present with all the strength of his desire, his fervor, his immediate physical enjoyment, with his imagination totally blocked by the violence of his exclusive passion and his absurd fidelity! Otherwise there's no longer asymmetry, but simultaneous absence, equilibrium, equity—and that's what must be avoided. In such cases, of course, reality is even better than fiction; a flesh-and-blood spectator is preferable to any imagined one. The lover's natural place is in the middle of the couple. Although the truth is that a real artist will always prefer *several* spectators to one."

"In other words," Emmanuelle said facetiously, "there's no eroticism without exhibitionism."

"I'm not even sure I know what that word means. But I do know, for example, that making love standing up, at night, in a street where a few strollers are passing by in their furs and silk capes, is something that stimulates the mind."

"Why not in broad daylight, in a crowded public square?" she asked ironically.

"Because eroticism, like all art, keeps away from crowds. It shuns jostling, noise, carnival lights, vulgarity. It needs small numbers, nonchalance, luxury, a proper setting. It has its conventions, like the theater."

Emmanuelle reflected. She was elated to find herself able to say suddenly, with sincerity, whereas she would have been inexplicably incapable of it a few seconds earlier: "I think I could do it."

"Make love in the street, before a few attentive passersby?"

"Yes."

"For the pleasure of making love, or for the pleasure of being seen doing it?"

"Both, I suppose."

"And what if you were asked to simulate it? If a man pretended to take you, would the sole pleasure of scandalizing people be enough for you?"

"No," she said resolutely. "In that case, what would be the good of it?" Realizing that she was also speaking for the present moment, because she wanted to make love immediately, because she wanted either to be taken by Mario or to masturbate in front of him, she did not know which (the choice was unimportant to her, provided her sex could be caressed), she added, "I also want a physical pleasure."

"Frequent orgasms? That's it, isn't it?"

"Of course, why not?" she admitted aggressively. "Is there anything wrong with that?"

"There may be." He let a few seconds pass, then stated:

"The pitfall of eroticism is sensuality."

"Oh, Mario, you're exhausting!"

"You mean I'm tiresome?"

"No. But you're too fond of paradoxes."

"That's not a paradox. You know what entropy is, don't you?"

"Yes."

"Well, then, entropy—that is, roughly, the attrition, the decline of energy—lies in wait for eroticism as it does for the whole universe. And the form of entropy that's peculiar to eroticism consists less in becoming inured to society than in satisfying the senses. A satisfied sexuality is a sexuality that's moving toward death. At every moment, in every individual, satisfaction threatens desire. It threatens it with a slack happiness, the satiety of eternal sleep. The only defense consists in refusing the temptation of satisfaction, in never being willing to have an orgasm unless you're assured of being able to have another one, or, rather, unless you're certain that, once your orgasm is over, you'll still be able to become excited."

"Mario . . ."

He raised his finger to request her attention. "What's erotic is not ejaculation, it's erection."

"What you advocate, then, on the pretext of eroticism, is depriving yourself of love-making, for fear it would make you have an orgasm! I think I'm going to stick to my original opinion —I don't give a damn about morality. Or about eroticism, either, if it requires so much virtue! I'd rather have as many orgasms as I want. And as many as I can. I'd rather give my body all the pleasure it loves. I don't want to measure myself out in little doses, even if it does give my mind some sort of perverse excitement!"

"Very good! If you only knew how much I approve of what you've said! What a joy it is to find a woman who's ready to devote herself entirely to pleasure! All the recommendations I've made to you have had no other purpose than to help you be more successful in doing just that. I haven't told you to mortify your senses or to measure out your pleasure. I'm telling you, 'If you want to enjoy erotic pleasure as much and as well as possible, if you want it to be a reward of your mind and not only of your flesh, respect these elementary laws: refrain from isolated sex acts that lead only to sleep; don't consider yourself contented for more than a few moments after an orgasm; try to have another one; don't let the ease of satisfaction win out over the exactingness of eroticism; don't imitate the mindless beatitude that concludes the sad coupling of animals; and don't confuse the idea of coitus with that of the couple."

He laughed.

"Think of it! You tell me I'm exhorting you to limit yourself when I'm actually opening the gates of the limitless to you! But you must realize that your horizon will always be shamefully restricted if you expect love from only one man. It's not the love of one man, or of a few, that I'm teaching you—it's the love of the greatest number!"

Emmanuelle thrust her lips forward in an expression of stubborn doubt and refusal that delighted Mario.

"How beautiful you are!" he exclaimed.

She shook her long hair and smiled at him. He smiled back with a look of esteem that she had never seen on his face before. She forced herself to speak, to thwart her emotion.

"So what must I do?"

"'Recline, O my body, in accordance with your voluptuous mission! Savor daily enjoyments and short-lived passions. Do not leave one unknown joy to the regrets of your death.'"

"That's just what I was saying!" she cried triumphantly.

"So was I."

She laughed, incapable of arguing. He always had to be right!

"But I was saying it in greater detail," he added.

"Too much detail!" she complained. "All your laws . . . I remember the first two . . ."

"I just gave you a third: the law of *number*. Multiplicity is in itself an element of eroticism. And conversely, there's no eroticism where there's limitation. Limitation to two, for example. I've already begun to explain my low opinion of the couple."

"We'll outlaw it," she agreed. "But where will that take us? Must I refuse to make love with one man at a time? Must I do it only in a trio, a quintet, a septet?"

"If you like. But not necessarily. Number exists not only in space, but also in time. And you're not limited to addition and multiplication. You can also divide and subtract. At the beginning of this evening I angered you by showing you one way, among many others, of dividing yourself. As for subtracting yourself, play occasionally at contending for yourself with your own senses. Before giving in to them, of course, keep them from reaching the fairy castle at the end of the enchanted road, make it move away from them as they advance. Make pleasure and desire endure. And don't intoxicate only yourself with your inaccessible charms. Give lavishly to some what you dole out sparingly to others, without either having deserved it. If a man believes he must languish for long months and struggle to conquer you like a Knight of the Holy Grail, give your body to him all at once, and completely, the first day. With a man to whom you've granted the most intimate caresses, often and for a long time, refuse 'the final gift' out of pure caprice. With a stranger, demand that he take you without precautions, but with a friend who since childhood has been dreaming of penetrating you gently, allow him to ejaculate only in your cupped hands."

"You're horrible! Do you really think I'll ever go in for that kind of debauchery? I'm glad you're only joking . . ."

"What is it in my suggestions that horrifies you? Is it the idea of using your hands?"

"Don't be silly! It's not that . . ."

"You do know how to use those wonderful instruments of lasciviousness, don't you?"

"Of course!"

"Good for you! So many women seem to believe that only their bellies, breasts, and mouths are endowed with powers. Yet hands make us human! Is there anything that can make a man more of a man than a woman's hand? He could fornicate with a doe or a lioness, caress her nipples or quiver beneath the softness of her tongue, but only a woman can make him ejaculate in her hand. In the name of humanism, that way of making love is worthy of being preferred to all others."

Emmanuelle made a gesture as though to signify that she granted all tastes an equal right to exist. One thought was troubling her, although she did not know exactly what obscure motives made her attach more importance to that one "law" of Mario's than to the others. She picked up the subject again:

"You may talk about dividing or subtracting myself, but what you're really suggesting is that I should give myself to a lot of people! This part of me to one, that part to another."

"And why shouldn't you let many lovers, an enormous number of lovers, share a body that's capable of taking pleasure from all of them? What objection do you have to that?"

"And why *should* I do it?"

"I've told you—for the sake of eroticism. Because eroticism needs *number*. There's no greater pleasure for a woman than to keep count of her lovers—as a child, on her ten fingers; as a young girl, in terms of school months and vacation months; as a wife, in the secrecy of her diary, marking with a mysterious sign each day when a new name has been added to the list. 'What? Nearly a month since the last one?' Or false remorse: 'This is terrible! Two in the same week . . .' Until she reaches the acceptance of triumph, the paean of pride: 'I've done it! A different one every day this week!' And whispered conversations with her best friend: 'Are you over a hundred?' 'Not yet. And you?' 'Yes.' Oh, pleasure, pleasure! Your body can contain a thousand, ten thousand other bodies! You'll regret only the lovers you didn't have. Remember the definition of eroticism that I gave you—it's the pleasure of excess."

Emmanuelle shook her head.

"You can't deny it," protested Mario, "since the law of numbers, if you look at it closely, is only a corollary of another law that I'm sure you've accepted—that you must avoid satisfaction. It's easy to understand why a plurality of amorous resources is essential to pleasure; lest your senses compromise and admit that they're satiated, don't give yourself to a man unless you're sure that after him there's another one ready to take you."

"But there's no reason why that should ever end!" exclaimed Emmanuelle. "After the second one there would have to be a third, and then still another in reserve."

"Why not? That's exactly what you have to strive for."

She laughed good-naturedly. "There are limits to human endurance."

"Unfortunately," he admitted somberly. "But the mind can go beyond them. What matters is that the mind must never be satisfied."

"The surest way to keep it alert, if I understand you correctly, would be to make love without ever stopping."

"Not necessarily," he said impatiently. "Making love isn't what counts, it's how you do it. The sex act in itself, even if it were repeated infinitely, could never be enough to create an erotic quality. If you give yourself to ten or twenty men in a row, it may bring you ineffable bliss—or sheer boredom. It all depends on the moment, on what occurred before and what you expect afterward. That's why, although there are laws, there are no rules. To reach erotic perfection you'll one day give yourself to twenty men in the same way, reproducing their flesh in you as if you were on a treadmill, letting them succeed each other in your body without even trying to tell them apart; another day you'll insist on taking your pleasure from each of the twenty in a different way."

"The thirty-two positions?" she asked sardonically.

"Absurd! Eroticism isn't a question of postures. It arises from *situations*. The only positions that matter are those of the convolutions of your brain. Make love with your head! Populate it with more organs and more voluptuous sensations than all the men on earth could give you. Let each of your embraces contain and announce all others. It's the presence, within the act, of past and future sex acts, of acts committed by others or with others, that will confer erotic value on it. And when a man takes you, it mustn't be he who gives the moment its charm; let it be the man beside you who's holding your hand or reading a page of Homer to you."

Emmanuelle burst out laughing, but she was more deeply impressed than she was willing to admit. "When my husband wants to make love with me, should I say to him, 'Impossible, there are only two of us'?"

"That would be a sensible attitude," Mario said seriously. "But, as I've told you, when the third party can't be there physically, it's your brain's duty to conjure him up."

This pleased Emmanuelle. Yes, really, she thought, it was the greatest pleasure she had known till now—that imaginary transfer to the arms of another man, chosen to suit her fancy, as soon as Jean penetrated her. She reflected that it was the first erotic discovery she had made on her own, and she had made it in the early days of their love, perhaps the fourth or fifth time he had taken her. At first she had granted herself that "extra" sparingly, at long intervals, as an exceptional reward. Then more often. Now, she told herself, practically every night. It was so good! Its frequency was a source of enjoyment in itself. She was always eager for Jean to make love, not only because of physical desire, but also because another man, the one she wanted at the moment, appeared immediately and she did not need to overcome any embarrassment, shame, principle, or convention in order to give him her most intimate and dissolute favors, to do with him in imagination what she might not have dared to do in reality. Since her pleasure was increased tenfold, so was Jean's, and thus she did not deceive him; on the contrary, each day she was a more ardent and sensual mistress for him. She promised herself that from now on she would systematically make love in that way, she would always evoke the "third partner" who was required for the observance of the law of asymmetry. She was so impatient at the thought of that refined pleasure that she wished Jean would take her at that very moment, so she could make love with another man. "With whom?" she wondered. Obviously not with Mario, that would be no fun. With Quentin.

"I'll have to be careful not to call two phantoms into my bed at once," she mocked. "That would make an even number and ruin the whole thing!"

Mario smiled. "No, it wouldn't. There would still be asymmetry, because the even number would be unevenly divided. It's true that I'll never encourage you to make love in a foursome, if it consists in coupling two by two, even in the same bed. There's nothing more insipid, more domestic. Leave that game to deserving bourgeois couples who like to indulge in it after vespers. But it would be unfortunate to conclude that the number four must be banished. It offers interesting possibilities, as long as you redeem it from the banality of the square and divide it, for example, into three and one. The same is true of eight, despite its evenness, because it can mean six men and two women, a very elegant combination which enables each woman to be served by three men at the beginning, and allows the two groups thus formed to be joined at the end."

Emmanuelle tried to visualize this arrangement.

"I admit," Mario said with a grin, "that simplicity also has its charms for a woman. The most delectable way of making love will always be, as you noted just now, to give herself to two men simultaneously." Emmanuelle raised her eyebrows, astounded at being credited with the idea. "There are few experiences more perfect and harmonious, and it's easy to understand why it's the favorite treat of any woman of taste. Between being taken by one man and being taken by two, there's the same gulf as between rice wine and Marc de Champagne."

He lifted the magnum and poured some of it into her glass. She took a sip of the bronze-colored liquid with a feeling of vague uneasiness. He kept his eyes on her.

"In the arms of a single man, a woman is already half forsaken. All the approaches to your senses have equal virtues and equal rights to be loved. And since one man can't be both at your beginning and at your end, let the two of them solve the dilemma of your body together. When their twin pleasure quenches the thirst of your ambiguous mouth, you know in its fullness the reason for being a woman, and its beauty." He asked courteously, "Do you like that?"

She looked down at the glistening sphere of her glass and coughed. He insisted, mercilessly: "I mean, do you like to make love with two men at the same time? Not just in imagination . . ."

She chose to be frank. "I don't know."

"Why not?" he asked with restrained surprise.

"I've never done it."

"Really? Why?"

She shrugged her shoulders.

"Do you object to that practice?" he asked with a touch of sarcasm.

Her face took on a series of expressions that were difficult to interpret precisely. He let the silence continue, and this increased her discomfort. She felt that she was on trial, guilty of some inexpiable sin against the mind.

"Why did you get married?" he asked abruptly.

At first, she did not know what to answer. She had the sensation of having been taken by the shoulders and spun around, as in a game of blindman's buff. Blindfolded, hands outstretched, she did not dare to step in any direction, for fear of falling into a trap. She did not want to admit to Mario that she had married Jean simply because she loved him—or even for the pleasure of making love with him. Then a more challenging idea occurred to her.

"I'm a lesbian," she said.

Mario blinked his eyes. "Good!" he said appreciatively. Then, suspiciously, "But are you still truly a lesbian, or was it only in your childhood?"

"I still am." As she said this, she was submerged by an unexpected wave of distress. Was she telling the truth? Would she ever be able to hold a woman's body in her arms again? In losing Bee, she had lost everything . . .

"Does your husband know about your tastes?"

"Naturally. So does everyone else. It's no secret. I'm proud to like pretty girls, and to be liked by them." She now felt a need to trumpet words of defiance. Yet they hurt no one but herself.

Mario stood up and paced the floor. He seemed enraptured. He came back to Emmanuelle, took her by the hand, sat her down on the sofa and knelt at her feet. To her surprise, he kissed her knees lightly, then put his arms around her legs.

"'All women are beautiful,'" he said with a fervor made striking by his deep voice. "'Only women know how to love. Stay with us, Bilitis! Stay! And if you have an ardent soul, you will see beauty as in a mirror on the bodies of your mistresses.'"

Emmanuelle thought with melancholy irony that it was just her luck to fall in love with a woman who looked down on lesbianism, and with a man who thought too highly of it!

Meanwhile he had already recovered his nonchalance. "Have you had many mistresses?"

"Yes, many!" She would not let the memory of Bee spoil that evening for her. "I like to change them often."

"And do you find as many as you want?"

"It's not hard. All I have to do is ask them."

"None refuse?"

"Very few!" she answered, but at the same time she was beginning to tire of putting up a bold front; she wanted to regain her simplicity and frankness. She corrected herself with a cheerful laugh. "There are some girls, it's true, who won't let themselves be conquered. But that's their misfortune!"

"Exactly," agreed Mario. "And you? Are you easy to conquer?"

"Oh, yes! I love to give in!" She smiled at her admission and added, "But only if my admirers are really pretty. I can't stand any girl who's not very beautiful."

"An excellent attitude," Mario complimented her. He then returned to a point which apparently fascinated him. "You say your husband knows about your feminine loves. But does he approve of them?"

"He even encourages them. Since I married him, I've had more mistresses than ever."

"He's not afraid that their caresses may turn you away from him?"

"What an idea! Making love with a woman and making love with a man are two different things. One doesn't replace the other; you need both. It's as sad to be purely a lesbian as it is not to be a lesbian at all."

This time Emmanuelle's opinion seemed categorical and her self-assurance appeared to impress even Mario.

"I assume that your husband also avails himself of your mistresses' charms," he said with respect.

She smiled roguishly. "Mainly it's my mistresses who dream of that."

"You're not jealous?"

"That would be too ridiculous!"

"You're right; sharing can only add to your pleasure." He nodded, apparently evoking delightful images.

Emmanuelle, for her part, pictured the bare bodies of her mistresses, so naked, so soft to touch, so beautiful! It was not certain that she had heard Mario's last comment.

"And what about him?" he asked, after a moment of silence.

She opened her eyes wide. "Him?"

"Yes, your husband. Does he procure many men for you?"

"What?" she said, profoundly shocked. "Of course not!" She felt herself blushing.

"Not even since your marriage?" he asked imperturbably.

She could not hold back a movement of indignation.

"In that case," he declared coldly, "I don't see what interest either of you has in being married." He sipped his brandy, savored it, and asked disdainfully, "Does he forbid you to make love with other men?"

"No," she hastened to answer, "not at all." Inwardly, she was not sure that she was not embellishing the truth.

"Has he told you that you could do it?"

She again felt that she was being prosecuted. "Not explicitly, of course. But he's never told me I couldn't. And he doesn't ask me whether I do it or not. He leaves me free."

Mario made a gesture of regret. "That's exactly what you ought to reproach him for. It's not that kind of freedom that eroticism needs."

She tried to understand what he meant.

"When you were alone in Paris and writing to him," he went on, "did you keep him posted on your lovers?"

Emmanuelle was overwhelmed by the awareness of her "banality." She shook her head, then tried to evade the question.

"I told him about my mistresses," she said.

He made a gesture which might have meant "That's at least better than nothing." They were silent again. She looked at Quentin. He was smiling with remarkable perseverence. She wondered if he really understood what was being said, or if his smile was merely intended to hide his boredom.

"But don't think Jean is jealous," she resumed, trying to erase the bad impression she knew she had made on Mario. "He's no more jealous than I am. He himself taught me to show my legs, for example. And it's to please him that I wear tight dresses, so that when I get out of a car my skirt will go up as high as possible. And even in the most proper drawing room, I sit very immodestly; you can check on it for yourself." She laughed. "Doesn't that show that he and I have some aptitude for eroticism?"

"Yes."

"He's the one who decides on my necklines, too. Do you know many husbands who uncover their wives' breasts so generously?"

"Do you also find it enjoyable to show your breasts?"

"Yes. But especially since Jean taught me to do it. Before I knew him, I liked to be touched—by girls, I mean—but I didn't care whether I was seen or not. I didn't get any pleasure from it. Now I do." She added bravely, "I wasn't born an exhibitionist—I became one! Thanks to him." And she insisted, "You see!"

"Have you ever wondered why your husband enjoys making you publicly desirable that way? If it's only to make you a sexual teaser, it's hardly praiseworthy. And if it's merely out of pride, to show off his wife's beauty as a kind of wealth, and taunt other men who are less rich in that respect, it's no better."

"Oh, no!" protested Emmanuelle, who could not bear to hear anyone speak ill of Jean. "That's not at all like him. He makes me show my body for the sake of others . . ."

"That's just what I was saying!" Mario exclaimed triumphantly. "If he does his best to make you stir up other men's lust, if he presents you that way to give them erections, it means that he wants you to make love with them."

"But . . ." she tried to object. This idea had never occurred to her and she could not think of anything that would help her to refute it. Yet she felt almost dazed. Was it conceivable that Jean expected that of her?

"After all," she pleaded, "why should he want me to deceive him? What kind of pleasure could a man get from having others possess his wife?"

"Come, come, my dear," said Mario, and his voice was stern, "are you still at that stage? Do you mean to say that you don't understand how, out of erotic refinement, a highly advanced man can want his wife to seduce other men? The author of *Ecclesiasticus* knew more about it than you do when he said,

'The grace of a wife delighteth her husband.' Be logical; if your husband is glad to know that you make love with women, why should he feel differently about men? Is there really such an essential distinction between heterosexual and homosexual love as you seem to think? As for me, I maintain that there's only one love, and that making love with a man or a woman, with a husband, a lover, a brother, a sister, or a child is all the same thing."

"But Jean has always known I liked girls, even before he deflowered me. I told him so myself, the first day I knew him," she added abruptly, picking up one of Mario's allusions. "And naturally, if I'd had a brother I'd have made love with him. But I'm an only child!"

"Well?"

"Well what? . . . What I'm saying is that when I caress a woman I'm not deceiving my husband."

Mario seemed amused. "Does he like men?"

"No!" The idea that Jean might be a homosexual struck her as absurd. Mario guessed what was in her mind.

"You're unjust," he pointed out.

"It's not the same!" He smiled and she was no longer sure it was not the same . . .

"Do you like him to go to bed with other women?"

"I don't know . . . I suppose so."

"Then why shouldn't he feel the same way about you and other men?" Emmanuelle thought, "Yes, why shouldn't he?"

"Another example," Mario went on, without waiting for an answer, "do you expose your legs and breasts merely as a matter of habit, or as a social game, or do you do it because it excites you to offer yourself?"

"Because it excites me, naturally!"

"Physically?"

"Yes."

"Is your pleasure greater when your husband is present?" She reflected. "I think so."

"When you're sitting sedately beside him and a man tries to see under your dress, don't you sometimes dream that he's also slipping his hands under it, not to mention the rest?"

"Of course," she laughed. This, however, did not convince her that Jean also enjoyed imagining the same scene.

Mario discerned it and sighed. "You still have a great deal to learn: everything that separates simple sexuality from erotic art." He returned to the attack, adding a tinge of irony to the word she had used: "If your husband didn't want you to 'deceive' him, why would he have let you come here without him this evening? Did he make any objection?"

"No. But maybe he thought that having dinner with a man didn't necessarily mean I was going to give myself to him." She was gracefully pretending to be natural. She did not know if her thrust had struck home.

Mario seemed lost in meditation. Just as she was beginning to let her thoughts drift toward other shores, he asked: "Are you ready to give yourself this evening, Emmanuelle?"

It was the first time he had called her by her name. She did her best to restrain the emotion she felt at hearing such a question asked so casually. She tried to make her answer equally casual, to prove her freedom: "Yes."

"Why?"

Embarrassment overcame her again.

"Do you give in to men easily?" he asked.

How unfair! Was the purpose of this conversation to humiliate her? She had to re-establish her worth.

"Not at all," she said with a vehemence that was unusual for her. "I told you I'd had many *mistresses,* I didn't say I'd had many lovers. To tell you the truth," she added, moved by a sudden impulse—and with some shame, for she disliked lying and did it as little as possible—"I've never had any. That will explain to you why I've never had anything to tell my husband on that subject—until now," she concluded, with a smile that was easy to interpret.

As she was attributing this virtue to herself she reflected that she was actually not far from the truth, for could she seriously give the name of "lovers" to those strangers who had possessed her in the plane? Marie-Anne had already said they did not count. And she herself had gradually come to doubt the reality of that adventure. In yielding to the waking dream that had been given to her between heaven and earth, she had been no more unfaithful than she was when she savored the immaterial embraces of the men to whom she abandoned herself in imagination while Jean took his pleasure in her body every night.

For the first time, she thought that perhaps she was pregnant by one of the travelers; she would soon know. But that was not very important either.

Mario, however, seemed to take a suddenly increased interest in her. "Are you joking? I thought I heard you say that you 'also' liked men."

"I do. Otherwise, why would I have gotten married? And I just told you, in so many words, that I'm ready to give myself to another man, this very evening."

"For the first time, then?"

She nodded to confirm her half-lie, then she thought with sudden anxiety, "Could Marie-Anne have told him my secret?" No, it was clear that Mario knew nothing.

"Maybe there have been other times when I was ready to do it, but no one took advantage of it *then*," she said with a grain of salt which he must have sensed, because he looked at her with a smile that she did not like.

He counterattacked: "Why do you want to deceive your husband? Is it because he leaves you physically unsatisfied?"

"Oh, no!" she cried, taken aback and suddenly unhappy. "Oh, no! He's a wonderful lover. I'm not at all frustrated, I assure you. It's not because of that. On the contrary . . ."

"Ah!" said Mario. "'On the contrary'? That's interesting. Would you mind telling me what you mean by that 'on the contrary'?"

She was furious with him. He had made an eloquent speech to demonstrate that Jean himself wanted her to have lovers, and he already seemed to have forgotten it . . .

But why, in fact, she asked herself, had she now so easily accepted the idea of being unfaithful? Why, for the first time in her life, and so abruptly, did she want to be a married woman who had a lover? Because that was exactly what she wanted— to be an *adulteress*. She wanted it, yet without loving Jean any less passionately—*on the contrary* . . . What was happening to her? She heard herself saying, before she had time to reflect on the meaning of her words: "It's because I'm happy. It's . . . it's because *I love him!*"

Mario leaned toward her. "In other words, if you want to deceive your husband, it's not because he bores you, or out of weakness, or to take revenge on him; *on the contrary,* it's because he makes you happy. It's because he's taught you to love what's beautiful. To love the wonder of physical pleasure given by the penetration of a man's body into the depths of yours. He's taught you that love is the dazzling of the senses that you feel when a man's nakedness crushes yours. That which gives life its constantly reborn splendor is the movement of your hands toward your shoulders to make your dress fall down to your waist and uncover your breasts, and the movement of your hands toward your hips to make your dress fall down to your feet and turn you into a statue more adorable than any dream. He's taught you that beauty is not in the guarding of your body, but in its offering; not in your waiting for other hands to undress you, but in the haste and freedom of your own fingers creating a reality more human than the heritage of matter."

Emmanuelle had been listening, not knowing if she ought to let herself be enveloped by the spreading branches of Mario's words, let them decide what she was . . . She looked up at him firmly.

"Is that how you'll give yourself?" he asked.

She nodded.

"And you'll tell your husband that he can be proud of you?"

She lost her serenity. "Oh, no!" she said in alarm; then, after a moment of hesitation, "Not right away . . ."

Mario's face took on an indulgent expression. "I see," he said. "But you'll have to learn to."

"What else do I have to learn?"

"The pleasure of telling; it's even more subtle, more refined, than the pleasure of secrecy. The day will come when even the savor of your adventures will be less precious to you than the voluptuousness of recounting them, with details that will excite you more than caresses, to the man who is both yourself and the most attentive of your spectators." He made a gesture of clemency. "But there's no reason to hurry. If, for the moment, discretion is easier for you, keep your husband in temporary ignorance of his pupil's progress." He smiled with a hint of mockery. "Anyway, it may be preferable to wait till that progress has become conclusive, don't you think? The way of eroticism is sometimes steep, *ad augusta per angusta,* but some day the very memory of your harsh labors will be sweet to you. Now you must decide freely. Are you ready to try everything?"

"Everything?" she asked cautiously. She remembered that Marie-Anne had spoken to her in the same terms a few days earlier.

"Yes, everything!" said Mario, suddenly concise.

She tried to picture what that "everything" might be—and succeeded only in imagining herself abandoning her body to Mario's whims. Since she had decided to give herself to him anyway, did it matter very much how he would take her? She even told herself, with a little irony, that her mentor had a rather exaggerated idea of the virtues of his amorous methods if he thought that the experience he was preparing for her would make her "mutate." Her previous experience with men was limited, she could not deny it, but even so she was convinced that to become capable of progress a woman had to do more than submit to the singularities of a lover. That male smugness amused her. But it did not irritate her enough to make her want to discourage it.

One thing did bother her, however—her inability to explain why, despite Mario's assurances, she preferred to have her affair with him remain unknown to Jean. It was not really for fear that Mario might have been mistaken about Jean's motives, she reflected. It was, rather, because she had glimpsed a short time earlier, without being able to express it clearly, that "deceiving" a husband whom one loved was a special, very tender pleasure; she had not thought of it before, but the temptation of it now made her temples throb with impatience. It was quite possible, she told herself, that in the world of eroticism the complicity of a woman's husband constituted a more advanced form of libertinism. But she had not yet reached that point. Before learning the complicated art that Mario had outlined to her, she wanted to content herself with something simpler. Did not adultery alone already offer her the possibility of marvelous discoveries? Did it not involve abstract eroticism as much as sensuality, since she was eager to *deceive* Jean as a matter of principle, to deceive him as much as she loved him, immediately, fully, with her whole body, with all her nakedness, with all the softness of her belly, into which a stranger's semen would flow.

Mario looked at her and his gaze embarrassed her. She changed position on the leather sofa, showing her legs as she had said she knew how to do. She told herself that he had probably talked to her about making love with two men at once because he wanted to share her with his friend. "All right, then," she thought, "I'll learn!" She would have preferred to deal only with Mario, or, if there was no way to avoid Quentin, to have him limit himself to the role of spectator, whose importance Mario appraised so highly. But she was determined not to oppose his demands. Perhaps, she acknowledged, she even had an obscure desire to be possessed by Quentin also. And since Mario claimed that making love with two men was so enchanting . . .

"Have you at least made love with several women?" asked her hero.

She marveled once again at his being able to read her thoughts so easily. He must know, therefore, how much she desired him. She saw him look at her legs and it made her forget to answer.

He said in the special vibrant tone that his voice always assumed when he quoted poetry:

> *"'I, so pure! My knees*
> *Foresee the terrors of defenseless knees!'"*

She was glad he was sensitive to the eloquence of her body. But he did not let himself be distracted from his curiosity so easily. He came back to his question: "I mean with several women at the same time?"

"Yes," she said.

He seemed overjoyed. "Aha, you're not so innocent!"

"Who said I was? I've never claimed any such thing."

Suspecting her of virtue had become the worst insult she could imagine. If showing her legs was not enough to make Mario respect her, she would stand up on the sofa and take off all her clothes. The impulse was so strong that she raised herself on her knees. And if that demonstration did not convince him, she would masturbate in front of him! Her breasts were burning with ardor; perhaps it was also the brandy that had suddenly made her so daring. But he remained nonchalant. He seemed more avid for verbal eroticism than for action . . . "And how do you go about it when you exchange caresses with two girls at the same time?"

Emmanuelle felt impatient. To hasten the end of his inquisition she described scenes in which imagination played a greater part than reality. She had no desire to probe her memories in detail, and a bit of invention, she thought, even if it was naïve here and there, ought to please Mario more than historical accuracy.

He was not taken in. "All that seems like child's play to me," he interrupted amiably. "It's time to grow up, my fair friend!"

Angered, she tried to deal her adversary a blow that would avenge her.

"And you," she said, "do you go about it better with boys?"

When she realized that such an inopportune allusion might thwart her own aims, she bit her tongue, but it was already too late.

To her surprise, however, he did not seem to feel the slightest embarrassment. On the contrary, his voice was infused with good humor. "We'll show you that, my dear!"

He said something to Quentin in English. Emmanuelle wondered in dismay if the two men were going to give her a demonstration on the spot.

6

The Sam-Lo

*In the morning sow thy seed, and in the
evening withhold not thy hand.*
                    —*Ecclesiastes*, 11:6

*The tree of knowledge enveloped her in
its foliage, which was my arms.*
            —Henri de Montherlant, *Don Juan*

The section of the city that Emmanuelle was now discovering bore little resemblance to the avenues lined with concrete buildings or villas shielded by the greenery of the gardens and the fiery glow of royal poincianas that she had known since her arrival in Bangkok. Was she dreaming, perhaps? The full moon gave the setting a pallor and an animated relief so well suited to the kind of ballet she was dancing that it seemed impossible for all that to be real. "Setting" was the right word, in its theatrical sense, with its evocations of false perspectives, platforms, cardboard walls, unstable assemblages and scaffoldings. Following Mario and followed by Quentin, she apprehensively placed one sharp-heeled shoe in front of the other on a footbridge made of a plank about thirty feet long and one foot wide, with each end resting on a support that rose from the still, greasy water of a canal that seemed to be primarily a sewer. Their weight bent it and made it rebound like a diving board. She had no doubt that sooner or later she would be thrown into the slime.

When they reached one support, they had to step sideways onto the next plank, which seemed even more rotten and shaky than the one they had just left. They had covered several hundred yards in this way, and there was no indication that their strange journey was about to end. The farther she went, the more Emmanuelle felt that she was leaving the known world forever. Even the air she breathed here had a different consistency and smell. The night was thick with such a total silence that she scarcely dared to breathe, much less to speak, as though for fear of committing a sacrilege. Finally she realized that this silence was actually composed of the shrill, even, uninterrupted chirping of crickets.

Half an hour earlier, she and her guides had left the log house in a narrow boat that, in answer to Mario's call, a boatman had brought to the floating pier. They had glided along the *khlong* for a long time. Then, without her being able to determine whether Mario had decided at random or recognized a landmark, they had left the boat and begun following that wooden sidewalk perpendicular to the main canal and above a secondary one that was narrower and apparently quite shallow, since the light Thai canoes could not use it.

This canal was bordered on both sides by low huts, with walls of rusty sheet metal or blackened bamboo and roofs of palm branches, connected with the footbridge by precarious drawbridges made of worm-eaten beams or unsquared logs. The doors and windows were carefully barricaded, as though closed against a plague. "How can they breathe?" wondered Emmanuelle. The sampan-dwellers' way of life made more sense to her: when she had passed their floating houses tied along the banks of the main canal, she had seen men, women, and children taking advantage of the rainless night, sleeping in the bow, under the stars, with their bodies pressed together, their mouths round and, sometimes, their eyes open. Why then should others lock themselves here in damp pits and shut out the slightest breath of air?

Her feeling of unreality grew more pronounced as time went by. It was incredible that their tightrope walk along this inhospitable street of stagnant water and dead wood could have gone on for so long without leading them anywhere. She was already dreading the acrobatics she would have to go through if she and her two escorts should happen to meet other nocturnal travelers coming toward them. She doubted that the problem would arise, however, because the realm into which her companions were taking her seemed too desolate to contain any living beings.

But a moment later a man emerged from one of the huts. Very tall, with a muscular torso the color of smoldering embers, wearing a piece of red cloth tied around his waist. He thoughtfully untied it, looking at the three foreigners who were walking toward him. When he was completely naked, he urinated into the water. Even in pictures, Emmanuelle had never seen a penis at rest that was as long as this one—as long in repose as Jean's in erection. "It's beautiful!" she thought. And the whole man was beautiful. When they came up to him, he stared at her from less than three feet away. She thought of only one thing—that penis. If it should rise . . . But the Thai remained as calm as marble. He looked at her half-bare breasts and his member did not move. They passed him and continued on their way.

A fork. The ghostly path branched out. Mario hesitated. He consulted Quentin and finally chose one of the branches. Emmanuelle was afraid it might not have been the right one, because they went on walking for a long time. But she did not dare complain. She had not said a word since they had left the boat. Suddenly a cry escaped from her. The wooden path had turned sharply and led into a kind of courtyard—she nearly thought it was a clearing because she had such a strong feeling of being lost in a jungle. Facing them was a fantastic figure, sixty feet high. She had seen it from a distance but had mistaken it for a tree. It was Genghis Khan—thick mustache, merciless eyes, hands grasping the daggers at his waist, bulging muscles softened by the moonlight. Emmanuelle's heart pounded in disorder. No doubt of it, the sorcery was beginning. In a moment, grimacing Mongols would burst out of their lair and make her the victim of bloodthirsty magic rites. While her imagination, swifter than her reason, was building a world of phantasms, a nervous laugh showed that she had not lost her head completely. Leaning against the gigantic conqueror's hip, looking like a miniature beside him, a ballerina in a tutu was smiling reservedly at the stars. Other figures of multicolored cardboard were piled up pell-mell, some standing, most lying on the ground.

"It gives you a strange feeling to run into those film advertisements in a place like this," Emmanuelle said, to reassure herself with the sound of her own voice. "I wonder how they could have been brought here—is there any other way than along this incredible footbridge?" She had a slight suspicion that Mario might have inflicted a useless trial on her.

"No," he said. He did not see fit to make any additional comments.

They crossed the storage area, passing between the great Khan's legs, walked along a corrugated iron fence, and entered a little courtyard. Yellow light was filtering from a half-open door. Mario stopped on the threshold, called out, then went inside without waiting for an answer. Emmanuelle was feeling less and less calm. It was a hostile place, impregnated with an odor that was difficult to define—something like a mixture of dust, smoke, licorice, and tea. They went into a windowless room containing only a bench covered with a torn cretonne.

A dirty curtain, dyed a hideous blue, was hung across its far end. Almost immediately, a hand pushed it aside and a woman appeared.

The sight of her relieved Emmanuelle a little. She was a very old Chinese woman—surely a hundred years old, thought Emmanuelle—whose perfectly oval face was so wrinkled that it looked like crêpe. Her skin color was like ancient ivory, almost orange. Her shiny white hair was carefully drawn back over her temples and tied in a bun. The slits of her eyes and lips were so thin that they could barely be discerned among the folds of her skin. Only when she began speaking in a cracked voice, uncovering black-lacquered teeth, was Emmanuelle able to determine with certainty where her mouth was. Her hands were hidden in the sleeves of her starched tunic, which seemed even whiter by contrast with the lustrous black silk of her broad trousers.

When she had finished a rather long speech, to which Mario appeared to pay no attention, the hostess made a low bow with an agility that was surprising, for she gave the outward impression that she was made of dry wood. Then she turned and plunged into the depths of the building. They followed her without a word. First they went through a totally dark room. Emmanuelle had a feeling that there were moving shadows in it. She was genuinely afraid. Next they entered a little room where she discovered with uneasiness that two old men, looking almost moldy, were lying naked on a varnished wooden platform. She blinked her eyes and had time to see their ribs outlined beneath their brown skin, spotted with white, and their dilated, dreamy pupils, which did not seem to see her. She also cast a quick glance at their wrinkled penises and dry testicles, but the group was already passing into another room, little different from the preceding one, except that it was unoccupied. The old Chinese woman stopped; this was where she had been taking them. She delivered another sermon, then vanished, as though through a trap door.

"What's happening?" Emmanuelle asked anxiously. "What was she chattering about? And what are we doing in this sinister place? Everything here is disgusting!"

"That's just an idea of yours," said Mario. "It's dilapidated, I'll grant you that, but it's well scrubbed."

Another woman appeared, much younger than the first, but also much uglier. She was carrying, on a round tray, an alcohol lamp with a long chimney an inch thick—Emmanuelle had never seen such massive glass, even in a lens—tiny little round tin boxes, long steel needles like those used for knitting stockings, dried palm leaves cut into rectangles, and an instrument that Emmanuelle could not identify—a tube of brown, highly polished bamboo, about as long as an arm and as thick as a flute. At first sight, it seemed to be closed at both ends, but then she saw that one end had a hole in it no wider than a matchstick. Its whole length was inlaid with silver-gilt motifs. About a third of the way up from the closed end, a kind of flattened wooden polyhedron, the size of her fist, seemed to be balanced on top of the tube, attached to it at a narrow point of contact. It was so polished and smooth that the dancing flame of the lamp was reflected from its surface in changing colors. At its center was a cavity that had the diameter of a pearl, with a very small opening at the bottom.

Mario anticipated his pupil's questions. "You're looking at a pipe, my dear. Isn't it a beautiful object?"

"A pipe?" she asked, laughing. "It doesn't look like one. Where do you put the tobacco? In that ridiculous little hole? It must not take long to finish smoking it."

"You don't put tobacco in it. It holds a little ball of opium. And you only take one puff, then you fill the bowl again. You'll see how it works when you've tried it for yourself."

"You're not going to make me smoke opium, are you?"

"Why not? I want you to know what that game—or that art—consists of, because you mustn't be ignorant of anything."

"And what if I . . . take a liking to it?"

"What harm would there be in that?" he laughed. "But don't worry; I haven't brought you here to convert you to opium. It will only be a prelude."

"And what will happen afterward?"

"You'll find out when the time comes. Don't be impatient, *cara*. The ceremony of opium requires perfect composure of soul."

"If I like it, can I come back?"

"Certainly," said Mario. Her questions seemed to amuse him. He looked at her with indulgence, almost tenderness.

"I thought it was illegal to smoke opium," she said.

"It is. And so is making love outside of marriage."

"What would we do if the police came here?"

"We'd go to jail." He pursed his lips and added, "But not without first having tried to bribe the policemen by negotiating your charms."

She smiled skeptically and teased him. "Since I'm married, I'm negotiable only at the cost of another crime."

"With God's help, you and the representatives of the law would commit that crime." He uncovered one of her shoulders and an entire breast; then, holding this breast in his hand, he asked, "Wouldn't you?"

Her face expressed doubt, but also happiness, because she was glad for him to undress and touch her.

"You wouldn't be willing to render that service for all three of us?" he said, scandalized.

She reassured him: "Yes, I would. And you know it . . ." Then, hesitantly, "And . . . how many policemen usually make those raids?"

"Oh, no more than twenty."

She laughed again.

The servant had put down her tray in the middle of the platform. Mario let go of Emmanuelle's breast, which she left uncovered, put his arm around her waist, and drew her forward.

"Lie down here," he said.

"Lie down? Is it clean? It doesn't look very well padded!"

"Why should the establishment go to the expense of buying a mattress when opium smoke is enough to round all

213

angles and make the hardest surface luxuriously soft? Besides, don't complain; wood is easier to keep clean than a mattress. Let that thought soothe your anxieties."

She sat down with repugnance on the extreme edge of the varnished platform while her two companions stretched out on either side of her, so that the three of them formed a circle around the lamp. After a few moments she overcame her disgust and followed their example by lying down and leaning on one elbow, with her head resting on her hand. She could not take her eyes off the oblong flame that was rising, without flickering, inside the thick, glass chimney. A kind of fascination emanated from it.

The Chinese woman knelt at the foot of the platform and opened one of the little boxes. It was filled with a dark, opaque substance that had the consistency of thick honey. With the point of one of the long needles, she took out a drop of it the size of a grain of wheat, held it above the lamp for an instant, rolled it on one of the pieces of fibrous leaf that she was holding in her other hand, and exposed it to the flame again. The scorched drop crackled, swelled to twice its size, took on beautiful glints and became so pure and shiny that the nearby objects were reflected in it, adorned with flames; it was oozing life.

"It's beautiful," murmured Emmanuelle.

She now felt that this sight alone was worth having come there. "I'll never get tired of looking at that little ball," she thought. "It's like a precious stone trying to say something. But no stone is that beautiful."

Twenty policemen, she remembered. That was a lot . . . But, to save Mario from jail, she knew she would do it.

She felt a pang of regret when the officiating priestess, who had finally given the drop of opium the shape of a little translucent cylinder, exactly proportioned to the bowl of the pipe, put it into the cavity with a deft movement and drew out the needle that had pierced it. Without wasting any time, she turned the bowl upside down over the lamp, almost touching the hot chimney. She held the stem of the pipe toward Mario; he put his lips to it and breathed in. The flame rose, charring the amber pearl. He drew the mysterious smoke into his mouth in what seemed to Emmanuelle an endless puff.

"Now it's your turn," he said. "Don't let the smoke come out your nose, don't choke, don't cough, breathe in slowly and steadily."

"I'll never be able to do it!"

"It doesn't matter; it's only to amuse you."

The woman prepared another pipe; again the brown sun blazed at the end of the magic wand, tumefying and panting as though from desire. Emmanuelle saw it as an image of her sex, calling with its swollen lips to the ram of fire that would traverse it, leaving it bruised, burned, and sated. It was pleasant, she thought, to feel her vulva becoming more moist as the iridescent drop expanded with pleasure above the flame. She liked that rite; it was as if she were preparing herself publicly, ceremoniously, to make love. She held her bare breast in the cup of her hand; she was happy. Only one thing was lacking in the scene to make it perfect: the attendant should have been a young, docile beauty with an innocent face and an offered body; Mario, Quentin, and Emmanuelle would slowly undress her by degrees, and play with her, together or in turn, each according to his tastes and to the extreme limit of his pleasure. What a pity that Mario had not provided for that! Emmanuelle nearly reproached him for it, but did not dare to do so. For a moment, however, she had such a strong desire for a girl's legs to be mingled with her own, and to have a girl's sex into which she could put her fingers, that the Chinese woman looked almost beautiful to her.

When the pipe was handed to her, she let the opium burn without breathing it in, so that there was no draft and the woman had to pierce the toffee-colored pearl again with her steel needle. At her second attempt, she succeeded in absorbing a thin puff. She laughed heartily.

"I like the taste," she said, "and I like the smell even more. It's a little like caramel. But it grates on your throat."

"You'd better drink some tea."

Mario gave an order to the servant, who stood up and soon returned with some very small funnel-shaped cups without handles, an earthenware teapot no larger than the cups, and a samovar of boiling water. The tiny teapot was filled to the brim with green tea. She carefully poured a jet of steaming water into it and immediately emptied its contents into a cup. The liquid had already taken on the color of copper. A penetrating fragrance arose from it, more like jasmine than tea. Emmanuelle burned her tongue and uttered a cry of pain.

"You must draw in air between your lips as you drink, to cool your tea," said Mario. "Or, more precisely, to be able to drink it hot without burning yourself. Like this."

He made a gargling sound.

"What terribly bad manners!" Emmanuelle said indignantly.

"In China, it's polite."

It was now Quentin who was smoking the pipe. He did not succeed as well as Mario.

"I want to try it again," Emmanuelle said impatiently, excited by the novelty of the experience. "I'm sure I'll have fantastic sensations this time. What will I dream about?"

"Nothing at all. In the first place, opium doesn't make you dream, it makes you lucid and frees you of all bodily miseries and mental fetters. Secondly, before you could feel any effect at all, you'd have to smoke several pipes."

"Then I will!"

"You'll have one more and that's all. If you went beyond that tonight, the only pleasure you'd get from it would be to have me hold your head while your stomach churned."

She was not too grieved by his prohibition, because her second pipe gave her a fit of coughing and did not taste as good to her as the first. As for Mario and Quentin, they both declined even a second experience.

"Are you afraid of becoming addicted?" she said mockingly.

"My dear," retorted Mario, "I'm going to tell you a very grave secret. Taken in excess, opium deprives its smokers of a large part of their male ardor. And, as you know, we haven't come here for the pleasures of the mind, but for those of the flesh."

"Ah, yes!" said Emmanuelle, with a new surge of uneasiness. She felt that this shabby setting was rather badly suited to the games of love, now that her desire had passed. And she wondered what role she was to play in it.

"You remember asking me how we went about it with boys, don't you? Well, the good lady who reigns over this clandestine opium den, with the majesty that you've seen, also raises comely young lads for the diversion of her clientele. We're going to ask her to present an assortment of them to us."

He said a few words to the servant. She hurried away and reappeared a few moments later with the wrinkled Chinese woman, who politely made her bows. Mario spoke to her briefly. She bowed again, then uttered a shrill yelp. The ugly girl who had prepared the pipes promptly stepped forward.

"The dowager speaks only Chinese—and an obscure dialect, at that," explained Mario. "She called the other woman to act as her interpreter."

"And what language do you speak to them in?"

"Thai."

He addressed their hostesses again. The conversation followed the complicated circuit and underwent the metamorphoses imposed on it by the situation. After a few minutes of this exchange, he reported: "She's answered my request by offering me something else. That's within the rules of the game."

"What did she propose?"

"Girls, of course. I made an appropriate remonstrance. Then she suggested showing us some salacious films."

"Well, why not?"

"We didn't come here for so little. She also offered to present a living spectacle—two maidens tenderly making love before our eyes. That's nothing that would interest you, is it, Emmanuelle?"

She contented herself with a pout that he could interpret as he wished.

He resumed his negotiations, then reported to them: "I told her we wanted some boys between twelve and fifteen years old, endowed with nimble tongues, classic buttocks, unfailing endurance, robust members, and rich sap."

Emmanuelle covered her breast. The old woman was looking at her insistently; she spoke again, in that rasping tone that gave Emmanuelle a shock each time she heard it. The servant translated and Mario replied with a single word.

"What did she say?" asked Emmanuelle.

"She wanted to know if the boys were for me or for you."

"And . . . what did you answer?"

"I said they were for all of us."

Emmanuelle felt as if the walls were turning a little. Was it the opium? No, Mario had said . . .

The old woman began droning again. She seemed to be as long-winded as Jeremiah; she bowed repeatedly and ended on a piercing note, raising her arms to heaven.

"I'm afraid things aren't going to work out," said Mario, even before the interpreter had opened her mouth. And a little later he confirmed it: "This old lunatic stubbornly persists in claiming that she has no boys available tonight. Some noble foreigners have allegedly ransacked her breeding-stock. Surely she simply wants us to pay her more."

He started the discussion again. She made more gesticulations of despair. He held firm. Finally, however, he announced: "She won't budge an inch. We'll have to seek our fortune elsewhere."

He conferred with Quentin for a long while.

"He insists on staying here," he informed Emmanuelle. "He says he's sure he'll eventually get what he wants. I doubt it, but that's his affair. I suggest that we leave him here and resume our stroll. What do you think?"

She was willing to go. The atmosphere of that place was becoming oppressive. Nevertheless, she felt an unexpected pang, almost a twinge of remorse, at the thought of leaving Quentin. "What's the matter with me?" she rebuked herself. "I regarded him as an intruder, a nuisance, when he came. I spent the evening being annoyed at his presence, except when I forgot all about it! We didn't say more than a dozen words to each other the whole time. And now I feel all stirred up and

weak about him! That's too much! I must be losing my mind"
. . . Even so, her heart was heavy when they left him there.

They walked past the blank-eyed skeletons.

"Those two don't appeal to you?" she asked Mario caustically.
She was still resentful of the two men for their insistence
on procuring boys for themselves. Couldn't they be satisfied with her, just for one night? Or, if they really didn't
like women, why did they both pretend to be so interested
in her? And that idiot Marie-Anne, how could she be so
featherbrained as to put her under the tutelage of homosexu-
als? When she got her hands on her again, she would make
her swallow her pigtails!

"Why is Quentin so fascinated with boys?" she attacked.
"It wasn't very nice of him to desert us like that."

She was about to add, with sudden rancor, that he had not
seemed so disgusted with women while he was caressing her
legs, but Mario did not give her time.

"For a man of taste, the love of boys will always have a quality that the love of women has only in exceptional cases—the
quality of *abnormality*. It, therefore, fits the definition of a
work of art that I recalled to you earlier this evening. For me,
making love with a boy is erotic insofar as it's against nature, as
imbeciles rightly proclaim."

"Are you sure it's not simply in *your* nature?"

"Yes, I'm sure. I like women. For a long time, going to bed
with a man was hard for me to conceive of. Then I made myself

listen to reason. I tried it for the first time last year. Needless to say, I was glad I did. As you can see, it took a long time for even *my* mind to develop!"

Emmanuelle was suffering from conflicting emotions. She wondered, in particular, how much of Mario's allegations she ought to believe. "And since your first experience, have you often practiced that . . . art?"

"I'm always careful to let things keep their rarity. *Bis repetita placent*—as you know, the opposite is true!"

"But," she insisted, "have you also loved women during the past year?"

He burst out laughing. "What a question! Do I look like a paragon of chastity?"

"Many women?" she wanted to know.

"Not as many, certainly, as the lovers I'd have had if I'd been lucky enough to be a pretty girl." He added, with a smile of homage to Emmanuelle, "And not as many as the mistresses I'd have had, either!"

This answer did not satisfy her; she became impatient. "Which do you like best?" she asked almost angrily.

Mario stopped. They had reached the place where the clearing gave way to the bridge of planks. He took her by the shoulders and drew her toward him; she thought he was going to kiss her.

"I love what's *beautiful*!" he said forcefully. "And what's beautiful is never something that's already been done and it's never something easy. It's something that you make out of life for the first time, with an act of yourself and the act of someone else, and that you throw toward the infinite before it has time to take on its dead form."

Man and woman—another world in the midst of the created world.

"What's beautiful is what didn't exist before you and wouldn't have existed without you and will never again be in your power when the injustice of death has felled you on this earth that you loved."

Haughty in their solitary knowledge. Strong in their exemplary designs.

"What's beautiful is the moment that was nothing and that you have made unforgettable. It's the person who was nothing and whose singular form you have lifted up against the amorphousness of destiny and the multitude."

Straying leaders leading astray, abolishing the map of ready-made roads.

"What's beautiful is to surmount your pieties toward your nation and your time, your fear of shocking them and being censured, so that a new species will be born of your refusal to be like your meek fathers, your faceless mothers, your hypocritical brothers, and your fashion-enslaved sisters."

They are different—but from what ugliness?
They are deviants—but from what stupidity?
They are strangers—but to what herd?
They are beaten—but for what a revenge!
They are exiled—but to what a future!

"What's beautiful is to hasten to discover, to make you leap without weighing the dangers or remembering past sweetnesses, it's doing what you've never tried before and will never experience again, because the days and nights of your life will be only those which you've enriched with an extraordinary act. And is there anyone in heaven or on earth who can give you back the days and nights you've lost?"

The moonlight petrifies them; the statue of Mario holds the image of a woman in its hands.

"What's beautiful is to try everything and refuse nothing, to be capable of knowing everything. Innumerable bodies in our likeness, men or women, 'heaven or hell, it matters not . . . to the depths of the unknown to find the new!'"

At the four corners of the crossroads, empty footbridges, straight, unreal, all alike.

"What's beautiful is what never has the same taste twice and has the taste of nothing else."

Black hair on bare shoulders between the condottiere's fingers.

"What's beautiful is to be the opposite of the gregarious, skittish, lazy animal that you were born."

The Tartar hero's burly figure hides the moon.

"What's beautiful is to refuse to let yourself stop, sit down, fall asleep, or look back."

The hours of the night have turned, the steel stars revolve out of sight in the brightened sky.

"What's beautiful is to say no to the temptation that immobilizes you, binds you, or limits you. And to say yes, always yes, however weary you may be, to the temptation that multiplies you and drives you forward and forces you to do more than is sufficient or necessary and more than others are content to do."

Yellow light from the half-opened door: shadows go in, shadows come out. Night without sleep.

"What's beautiful is to find a new cause of astonishment every day, a reason for wonder, a pretext for effort and victory over the temptation of the acquired and over the satiation and sadness of age."

My heart opens to your voice . . .

"What's beautiful is to *change,* tirelessly. Because every change is an advance, every permanence a grave. Contentment and resignation are a single despair, and anyone who stops and gives up becoming something else has already opted for death."

The gong of a temple, muffled by the din of the insects.

"You're always free, of course, to prefer the peace of tombs, to embalm yourself in the mediocrity of an existence without desires, like a wax virgin in her jeweled shrine."

Two children emerge from the shadows and walk by, hand in hand.

"But I, who am trying to win you over not to death but to life, I say that it would then be better if you had never been born. Because each human life that becomes frozen is a dead weight on our planet, and hinders the advance of our species."

They are brother and sister. They are going to make love.

"Know this, Emmanuelle: the future of the earth will be what your body's power of invention makes it. If your dream should darken and your wings fold, if, by a stroke of misfortune, your curiosity should falter, your insight and perseverance should fail, then that will be the end of Man's hopes and chances: the future will be eternally like the past."

The white ballerina between the warrior's legs.

"Love of loving is what makes you the fiancée of the world. Thus everyone's fate depends on your passion and courage, and if you forgo the conquest of a single man or a single woman, you, their betrothed mistress, will be enough to make the race forgo the conquest of the light-years and the nebulae."

Mario's voice silences the song of the crickets.

"Do you understand? It's not the pleasure of the moment that I bring you, but the pleasure of the most remote. Happiness is not in the place where you are, it's in the place you dream of reaching."

In increasingly numerous arms.

"Ah, yes, Emmanuelle! I don't quench your thirst with illusions, I burn you with reality!"

At the center of the triangle formed by the stars Alpha of Boötes, Alpha of Libra, and Alpha of Virgo.

"I teach you not that which is most convenient, but that which is most daring."

"Take me," said Emmanuelle. "You don't know me yet; I'll have a new taste for you." She was surprised to see so much esteem in Mario's eyes.

He shook his head. "That would be too easy. I want something better. Let me guide you." He pushed her in front of him. "It's time to become an acrobat again!"

She submissively walked ahead of him. When they came to the fork in the road he decided that they would take a path other than the one by which they had come.

"I'm going to show you something out of the ordinary," he promised.

They soon came to the edge of a wide *khlong*—or was it a natural stream? It seemed to be winding. Its banks were covered with grass.

"Are we still in Bangkok?"

"Right in the middle of it. But this place isn't known to foreigners."

They began walking across a meadow, and because Emmanuelle's heels sank into the soft ground she took her shoes off.

"You'll tear your stockings," said Mario. "Wouldn't you rather take them off?"

She appreciated his thoughtfulness. She sat down on the trunk of a fallen tree. She pulled up her skirt. The cool air reminded her that her panties were in Mario's pocket. The moonlight was so bright that her belly could be seen clearly while she was taking off her garter belt.

"I never tire of the beauty of your legs," said Mario. "The beauty of your long, lithe thighs . . ."

"I thought you quickly tired of everything."

His only answer was a smile. She did not feel like moving.

"Why don't you also take off your skirt?" he suggested. "You'll be able to walk more easily. And I'll enjoy seeing you that way."

She did not hesitate an instant. She stood up and unfastened her belt.

"What shall I do with it?" she asked, holding her skirt in her hand.

"Leave it on the tree, we'll get it when we come back. We'll have to come this way in any case."

"What if someone steals it?"

"Would that matter? You wouldn't have any objection to going home without it, would you?"

She did not argue. They continued on their way. Below her black silk sweater, her buttocks and legs, despite their tan, looked strangely bright in that night. Mario was walking beside her; he took her hand.

"We're there," he said after a time.

A crumbling wall rose before them. He helped her to climb up on the bricks and jump down on the other side. When she looked up, she started. A human figure was crouching nearby. She gripped Mario's hand.

"Don't be afraid. They're peaceful people."

She almost said, "But I'm half-naked!" Once again, fear of his sarcasm held her back. But she was so ashamed that she felt incapable of taking a single step. She would have been less embarrassed if she had been completely naked. He led her forward inexorably; they passed close to the man, who looked at them with burning eyes. She could not help shuddering.

"Look," said Mario, pointing, "have you ever seen anything like it?"

She looked in the direction of his gesture. From a tree with an enormous trunk, veined with countless roots and wild vines, strange objects were hanging like fruit. When she focused her eyes on them, she saw that they were phalluses. She uttered a rather admiring exclamation.

"Some are votive offerings," explained Mario, "others have been hung in the hope of obtaining fecundity or sexual potency. Their size is in proportion to the worshiper's wealth—or the urgency of his prayer. I must point out to you that we're in a temple."

This reminded Emmanuelle of the indecency of her attire. "If a priest should see me like this . . ."

"You don't seem at all out of place to me, in a sanctuary dedicated to Priapus," said Mario, laughing. "Everything connected with his cult is permissible, even respectable, here."

"Are those what are called 'lingams'?" asked Emmanuelle, whose curiosity was stronger than her embarrassment.

"Not exactly. The lingam is Hindu and its design is generally stylized. It's often a mere pillar stuck in the ground, and it takes the eyes of faith to identify what it represents. Here, as you can see, the object is fashioned in such a way as to leave nothing to the imagination. These are replicas of nature, rather than works of art."

The phalluses hanging from the branches ranged from the size of a banana to that of a bazooka, but the realism of detail was the same in every case. They were all made of carved and colored wood, with a little spot of pink to embellish the opening at the tip. The foreskin was figured by deep folds behind the glans. The arched shape of the erection was rendered with striking beauty.

Hundreds of them were hanging from several other trees. Wax candles had been placed here and there, in wooden candlesticks, all through that penis orchard. Most of them were extinguished, but numerous sticks of incense, identical to those which one lights before the image of Buddha or on the altar of one's ancestors, were burning in the garden, giving off their heady, tenacious odor. Their glowing ends dotted the night with little points of red.

Emmanuelle saw with anxiety that several of these sticks were moving. The night was so light that it did not take a great effort for her to ascertain that they were held by human hands. It was not one man who was there, but four, five, six, at least ten men. Sitting on their heels, like the first one she had encountered. One of them stood up. She saw him approaching. When he was a few steps away, he crouched again. His eyes expressed calm, steady interest. Almost immediately, two, then four others joined him and squatted beside him. One of them looked very young, nearly a child. The others were older. None of them said anything. They continued holding their fragrant sticks between their joined fingers.

"Here's a sympathetic audience," Mario said jokingly. "What shall we perform for them?"

He plucked a phallus, of relatively modest size, from the nearest tree.

"I don't know if I'm committing a sacrilege," he said, "but if so, I'm committing it boldly. In any case, they don't seem offended." He handed the carved wood to Emmanuelle. "Isn't it pleasant to touch?" She felt it. "Show them how you would use your hands to do honor to it if it were alive."

She complied without protest, and even with a certain relief, because for a moment she had been afraid he might ask her to use it as a dildo and put it inside herself. She was revolted by the thought of its roughness and dirtiness.

Her fingers caressed the religious effigy as though they really hoped to make it ejaculate. She herself was finally taken in by that parody. She almost regretted not being able to use her lips, but the instrument was really too dusty!

She was aware that the men's eyes had begun to glow. Their faces were rather tense. Mario made a movement. Almost immediately she saw his erect penis, larger and redder than the wooden phallus.

"It's now time for illusion to yield to reality," he said. "Let your hands be as tender to flesh as they were to inanimate matter."

She put the article of worship in the hollow of a branch—she did not dare drop it on the ground—and obediently took hold of his member. He turned to face the squatting men so that they could see better.

Time stopped. No one made a sound. She remembered the "humanism" Mario had preached to her in his house on the *khlong,* and she concentrated to the point of dizziness.

She no longer knew if the pulsations in her hand were his or those of her own heart. She also recalled his precept—*endlessly!* And she made miraculously artful efforts to *make it last.*

Finally he murmured, "Go!" At the same time, he turned toward the tree from which the priapic fruit was hanging. A spurt of uncommon length and density traversed the night and sprayed some of the wooden phalluses, making them swing and turn at the ends of their vines.

"Now you must do something for our spectators," he said immediately. "Which of them appeals to you most?"

Terror made her speechless. No, no! She could not touch those men, she did not want them to touch her . . .

"Isn't the bambino adorable?" said Mario. "I myself wouldn't mind being tempted . . . But tonight I'll leave him to you."

Without consulting her any further, he motioned to the boy and addressed a few words to him. He stood up slowly and with dignity and came over to them, not at all intimidated; he seemed, in fact, rather disdainful.

When Mario had said something else to him, he took off his shorts. Naked, he was more beautiful, and this comforted Emmanuelle in the midst of her agitation. A still-juvenile penis was thrust out horizontally in front of her.

"Suck and drink," Mario ordered in a matter-of-fact tone.

She had no thought of refusing. She was, moreover, in such a state of confusion and turmoil that her acts themselves no longer seemed to have any great importance. She merely told herself that she would have preferred the naked man they had passed earlier, on the bridge of planks . . .

She knelt on the soft, thick grass and took the boy's member in her hand, pushing back the skin that half covered its end, which quickly grew larger. She put it between her lips, as if she first wanted to taste it. She kept it there for a moment while her hand slid along the rest of his penis. Then, with sudden resolution, she took all of it in her mouth, so deeply that her lips touched his bare belly and her nose sank into his sparse down. She remained motionless for a time, then, conscientiously, skillfully, without trying to cheat or hasten the end, she began moving her mouth back and forth.

This test, however, was an ordeal for her, and for the first minute she had to struggle against a nausea that rose in her throat. It was not that she felt it was degrading, in itself, to perform that act of love with an unknown boy. The same game would have pleased her greatly if Mario had imposed it on her with a blond, elegant boy who smelled of *eau de cologne,* in the bourgeois drawing room of a Parisian friend. She had, in fact, come very close to deceiving Jean for the first time— without the feeling of deceiving him, because with a child it would have seemed like a joke—just before she left Paris, by giving in to the advances of the precocious little brother of one of her mistresses! They had been disturbed a minute too soon, but she had already given her consent, not only mentally but very physically . . . The opportunity had not been repeated; she thought of it now, and reflected that, all things considered, she was rather naturally dissolute. Since then, she had made imaginary love at least a dozen times with that little boy who had known nothing of her but a moist, offered sex, and had begun to penetrate it. But with this one it was not the same. He did not excite her at all. On the contrary, he frightened her. Furthermore, she had at first been repelled by the thought that he might not be clean; fortunately she was now reassured, and she belatedly remembered, with relief, how thoroughly the Thais wash themselves several times a day. Even so, this experience gave her no pleasure. She was going through with it to obey Mario, but her senses and her inclinations refused it.

"Do a good job anyway!" she told herself almost violently. A kind of pride urged her to treat the boy in a way that would leave him an indelible memory. Jean had told her that there was no other woman in the world who could make her mouth serve love so well . . .

Little by little, she let herself be caught up in her own game. She forgot to whom that penis belonged and began loving its warmth and strength, letting its glans probe her throat and seek, to suit itself, the place where it would climax its excitement. She felt her lips and her clitoris becoming sensitive; she finally closed her eyes and let her sensations take hold of her. When her caresses reached their goal, the flood of sperm on her tongue gave her as much pleasure as if it had been Jean's. It had a different taste; she found it very good. It did not matter that all those men were looking at her; she wanted to bring her own excitement to fruition. Before the boy had withdrawn his penis from her mouth, she began stroking the bud of her sex with her fingertips, and a short time later she abandoned herself to orgasm in Mario's arms while he kissed her lips for the first time.

"Didn't I promise to let you give yourself bit by bit?" he said when they had climbed back over the ruined wall. "Are you happy?"

She was. But she was still not delivered from her embarrassment. She remained silent.

"It's very important for a woman," he commented thoughtfully, "to drink sperm often, and from many and varied sources." His voice suddenly became ardent: "You *must* do all that because you're beautiful."

"Isn't it possible to be pretty and remain decent?" she sighed.

"It can be done, of course, but at one's own expense. Is it forgivable for a pretty woman not to use the power of her beauty to obtain what homely women vainly long for all their lives?"

"You seem to think that all women dream of nothing but debauchery."

"Is there any other good?"

No one had stolen her skirt. She put it on and missed her previous comfort. They again took a direction different from the one she knew. She wondered if they were going to walk much longer. As she was getting ready to complain, they came to a real street.

"We'll take a *sam-lo,* if we can find one," said Mario.

She had never used that means of transportation, which had become rare, and she liked the idea of trying it. It would be more enjoyable to let herself be carried along by the indolent rhythm of a tricycle rickshaw under the luminous sky than to risk death at every turn in a taxi. They walked several hundred yards along the street before they found an available *sam-lo.* Its driver—also called a *sam-lo,* as if he were an integral part of his vehicle, explained Mario—was meditatively sitting on the ground. As soon as he saw them, he made a gesture of invitation toward the narrow seat covered with red oilcloth.

Mario had a brief discussion with him, probably to agree on the amount of the fare, then motioned Emmanuelle to get into the *sam-lo* and sat down beside her. Although they were both remarkably slender, they were squeezed in tightly. He put his arm around her shoulder and she pressed up against him, happy. In sitting down, she had pulled her skirt up to the tops of her legs, because he had told her he liked them. The *sam-lo* began pedaling his rickshaw. She suddenly had an idea that she herself judged to be fantastic and insane. She had never done such a thing of her own accord, and, still worse, in public, out in the street! But she was going to do it. She gathered up all her courage.

She turned sideways a little, toward Mario. With one hand, which she tried to make firm, she undid one of his buttons, then, hastily, all the others, moving downward. She slipped her hand inside his trousers and took hold of his sleeping penis. Only then did she begin breathing again.

"That's good, Emmanuelle!" he said. "I'm very proud of you."

"Really?"

"Yes. Your act deserves to be admitted into the kingdom of eroticism, because convention requires men to take the initiative and women to follow their lead. A woman who makes the first move, at a time when a man isn't expecting it at all, creates an erotic situation of the highest value. Bravo!"

She felt in her hand that his approval was not purely moral.

"Remember that principle in other circumstances," he went on, "and you'll always find it to your advantage. Needless to say, however, it's subject to the clause of novelty, according to the rule."

"What do you mean?" she asked. She began caressing him gently.

"If you're a gentleman's habitual mistress and you take off your clothes in front of him, even if he hasn't asked you to, there's nothing unexpected in it. And therefore there's no eroticism in it. But if your ambassador introduces you, during lunch, to a diplomat who's passing through Bangkok, and asks you to take him to see the temple of the Reclining Buddha; and if, afterward, having invited him to have a cup of tea in your parlor, to refresh himself after his guided tour of the city, you sit down beside him on your best white silk sofa and casually take off your blouse, shaking your hair in a perfectly natural way, that spontaneous act will leave an imperishable mark in his memory. On his deathbed, his last thoughts will be of you, and it will be your image that comes to haunt him and console him. After that beginning, of course, a whole range of possibilities is open to you. Or you can provisionally stop there and, with your breasts bare, ceremoniously pour him a cup of tea, without neglecting to ask how many lumps of sugar he usually takes. There's a good chance that he won't be able to remember. That, moreover, is how you'll know what's most appropriate to do next. If he answers 'eight,' or 'fourteen,' or 'an inch,' don't expect him to take the next step; give him two lumps and move closer to him. Then proceed as you've just done with me and ask him whether he prefers to ejaculate before or after drinking his tea, and where—in your hand, your mouth, or his cup. What happens from then on doesn't matter much. The climate has been created. And the masterpiece, as you like to say, is off to a good start. If, on the other hand, your visitor still has some semblance of composure, leave it to him to do the right thing, that is, to grab you and behave like the wild beast that you've unleashed in him; it will be entirely to your benefit.

"On another occasion, for the sake of variety, you'll take off not only your blouse, but all your other clothes as well, without ever losing your urbane manner or showing even the most fleeting emotion. When you've taken hold of your skirt with your left hand, stepped out of it with your long ballerina legs and sedately dropped it onto a footstool, and when you've taken off your panties, if you're wearing any, and safely tucked them away in the vase of orchids, you'll sit down again to the left of your visitor and lean back on the cushions of the sofa with a gracious smile. If he turns out to be paralyzed with astonishment, you'll tell him, to put him at ease, how you were raped the day before by two plumbers armed with wrenches, and how much pleasure you got from it. Give him a long description of your tormentors' organs and the liberties they took with your body. If he still doesn't move, masturbate in front of him.

"And finally, on a third occasion, with another distinguished visitor, you won't undress, but as you're lifting the teapot, and before asking him about the sugar, you'll say to him quite simply, 'Shall we make love after we've had our tea?' If, by any chance, he should decline, on the pretext of an old wound, a vow he made at the bedside of his Carmelite godmother, or an article of the Code of Hammurabi that forbids ejaculation before sundown, you'll answer in a proper tone, without showing any resentment, 'You're right. I can't imagine what came over me just now. When I married my husband I promised to be faithful to him, and since I've never deceived him it wouldn't be fitting for me to begin today.' The imbecile will be desolate at having missed his chance to have the rare pearl that you are. If he changes his mind, be intractable. If he tries to abuse your innocence, call the police and see to it that he's given the maximum sentence. No jury will give credence to the wild assertions he'll make in his defense—the truth!"

Emmanuelle was delighted by the size to which Mario's member had grown as the result of her nursing. Nevertheless, she said to him, without trying to attenuate her sarcasm: "If I remember correctly, Professor, I made a similar offer to you less than an hour ago. Since you've insultingly rejected me, I'm going to turn you over to the first policeman I see."

He gave her a kindly smile. "I adore your hand; don't change your way of using it. My dear, you mustn't try to make yourself seem more foolish than you are. You know very well that our relations have nothing in common with the situation I've described to you."

She could not see where the difference lay, unless it was in the absence of tea. But she was in no mood or condition to argue: the caresses she was giving him had inflamed her own senses; even the jolting of the springless rickshaw on the rough street added to her pleasure.

"The *sam-lo* doesn't know the sight he's missing," remarked Mario.

He whistled. The *sam-lo* turned around; his eyes went from one of his passengers to the other, and brightened with a broad smile.

"He likes us," noted Emmanuelle.

"Yes, we've found an accomplice. It's not surprising, because he's handsome. There's an international freemasonry of beauty. A certain number of things are permitted only to those who are beautiful. Montherlant once pointed out quite rightly, in a letter to Pierre Brasseur, that 'licentiousness is not at all vulgarity; it is prudishness that is vulgarity.'"

"Courteline said it before him: 'True modesty consists in hiding what is not beautiful,'" quoted Emmanuelle, rather proud of her erudition.

"Are you ashamed of your breasts, then?"

"Oh, no!" With the hand that was not caressing Mario, she pulled her sweater out of her skirt and began taking it off. He helped her. For a moment she had to let go of his erect organ, but it was only a brief interlude.

"Now I wish we'd meet someone," he said.

"Isn't the *sam-lo* good enough as a witness?" she pleaded, in spite of herself.

"He's no longer a witness, he's a participant."

He whistled again and the Thai looked back from his saddle. He seemed keenly affected by Emmanuelle's near nakedness and the rickshaw swerved sharply. All three laughed loudly. Emmanuelle felt as if she were a little drunk. It was too late for it to be the effect of the brandy.

Mario's wish was granted. A car passed them and slowed down abruptly. Emmanuelle thought it was going to stop and her heart skipped a beat. But it went on. It had been impossible to distinguish the faces of the occupants.

"Some of your friends, perhaps?" Mario suggested cruelly.

She made no reply. Her throat was constricted. She preferred to think only of caressing him well. Another rickshaw came toward them, with two American sailors crowded into it. They screeched like peacocks when they discovered the spectacle. Mario and Emmanuelle pretended not to see or hear them. The sailors gesticulated desperately, trying to stop the two vehicles, but neither driver showed any reaction and they both continued pedaling at a steady rate.

"I'm sorry there's no cup," Emmanuelle said. "Where would you prefer to ejaculate, in my hand or mouth?"

Mario did not answer immediately. She leaned down and took him first between her lips, then deeply into her mouth. She heard him reciting:

> "'Continue till I say to you,
> "Alas, I can't hold back, my love!
> Alas, dear God, I can't hold back!"
> Then withdraw your little mouth
> To let me, dying, heave a sigh
> Before you bring me to the end.'"

Curiosity made her interrupt her work; she straightened up and asked, "Did you make up that amorous poem?"

"Absolutely not. It's from *La Première Journée de la Bergerie,* by one of your sixteenth-century compatriots, Rémy Belleau."

"Good heavens!" she said, laughing.

Before she had time to get back into position, they stopped in front of the gate of Mario's garden.

He slipped away from her hands, leaped out of the rickshaw, and buttoned his trousers. She also got out, but did not judge it necessary to put on her sweater; she held it in her hand, along with her purse. Her breasts showed an admirable curvature in the moonlight.

He opened the gate. The *sam-lo* was now standing beside his rickshaw with no visible emotion, apparently waiting to be paid. All at once, Mario jumped onto the seat and swiftly pedaled the vehicle into the garden before the Thai could make a move. Emmanuelle and the *sam-lo* looked at each other and burst out laughing at the same time. He was not at all upset by Mario's prank; for the moment, in fact, he seemed much more concerned with admiring Emmanuelle's contours than with recovering his property. She was the first to go after the runaway. She found him standing in front of the log steps of his house, exultant, holding the rickshaw by the handlebars.

"What a madman you are!" she reprimanded him tenderly.

"I also love your breasts," he said, as though announcing a decision that he had reached after long reflection.

"I'm lucky!"

She was more flattered than she was willing to admit. The *sam-lo* rejoined them, smiling, and without haste. Mario spoke to him—a real speech, with intonations, silences, and eloquent effects. She wondered what he could be saying. The *sam-lo*'s face showed nothing that she could use as a basis for conjecture. Suddenly he replied, looking at her at the same time. Mario resumed his discourse. The Thai nodded.

"There, it's settled, and I've found my hero!" said Mario. "Another example of how a man will sometimes go far away in search of what he could easily have found in front of his door!"

"What? Do you mean . . ."

"Of course. Don't you deem him worthy of my favors?"

This time, Emmanuelle felt almost on the verge of weeping. Mario's graciousness during their ride had made her forget his previous rebuffs. More or less consciously, she had been expecting him to take her in his arms as soon as they were inside his house. She was ready to spend the rest of the night there if he asked her to, and had given up all thought of going home. He could have done with her whatever he wanted, and now it turned out that he wanted nothing! The only thing he had in mind was to find a young man for his bed! She looked at the *sam-lo;* her eyes were so blurred with tears that she could not see him distinctly. Was he really so handsome? She recalled having thought that he had the face of a boxer . . .

"Don't begin tormenting yourself in advance again, *cara!*" Mario said gaily, interrupting, as usual, her somber reflections. "I have a marvelous idea, you'll see. Once again you'll be grateful to me. Come in, hurry."

He opened the door and drew her inside, holding her by the waist. She yielded to him without ceasing to sulk. She had had enough of his ideas. Even so, she was glad to return to the drawing room with its areas of light and shadow, the red leather sofa, and the spicy smell of the *khlong*. There did not

seem to be many boats passing now. It was so late—or so early!
She suddenly felt sleepy. What a night!

Mario brought enormous glasses containing crystals
sparkling in a green liquid. "Peppermint on the rocks," he
announced. "That will put new life into my beloved!"

His beloved? The word brought a faint, bitter smile to
her lips. The *sam-lo* was standing rather stiffly in the middle of the room. He took, with obvious embarrassment, the
glass that Mario handed him. They all three drank in silence.
Emmanuelle was so thirsty that she emptied her glass all at
once. Mario was right; she felt herself reviving. He abruptly
sat down beside her, put his arms around her, and kissed her
left breast.

"I'm going to take you," he said. He waited to judge the
effect of this declaration.

She was too stunned to show any reaction. Furthermore,
she was not convinced.

"But I'm going to take you through this handsome faun.
I'm using the word 'through' in its literal sense, that is, I'm
going to traverse him to reach you. I'm going to possess you
as you've never been possessed before, and as I've never before
possessed a woman. You'll belong to me more than anyone has
ever belonged to anyone else. Do I have your consent?"

She did not understand what he meant, or perhaps she was
unwilling to understand. But it did not occur to her for an
instant that she should or could refuse. Whatever Mario asked

of her was right, and she accepted it. The only thing she had dreaded was that he might ask nothing of her.

"Do whatever you like with me," she said.

For the second time, he kissed her on the lips. Now she was completely happy. And impatient for him to exercise his power over her.

"Your first lover!" he said elatedly. "You're going to have your first lover tonight!"

She was ashamed of having deceived him, of not having admitted her adventures in the plane to him. But was it important? In a sense, because for the first time she was giving her entire consent, because with total lucidity, with full awareness, with premeditation, she *wanted* to be an adulteress, he really would be her first lover.

"The first of many?" he asked, as though to be make sure she had assimilated his teachings.

"Yes," she answered.

How wonderful it was to abandon herself so completely! A woman who gave herself to only one man could know nothing of the step that Emmanuelle was now taking in promising all of herself to many men, an unlimited number of men. No other woman could ever be as adulterous as she was at that moment. Who else could perform the miracle of deceiving her husband, for the first time, with all the men who would want her in the future?"

"You'll never refuse yourself again?" he insisted.

She shook her head. She thought, "If he orders me to give myself to ten men tonight, I'll do it."

He asked her to give herself only to the *sam-lo*. She took off her skirt and remained on the sofa, leaning back against the thick cushions, whose softness delighted her. She held her legs apart, with her heels resting on the rug, and put her arms around the *sam-lo*'s back as he cautiously began penetrating her. When he was completely inside her, Mario, who till now had been sitting next to her, embracing her, stood up and placed himself behind the *sam-lo*. His hands seized him by the sides and she felt them touching hers.

She heard moans of pleasure escaping from Mario. Sometimes they were almost shouts.

"Now I'm in you," he said. "I'm piercing you with a sword twice as sharp as that of common men. Do you feel it?"

"Yes. I'm happy."

The *sam-lo*'s hard penis withdrew three-quarters of its length from her, returned inexorably, and resumed its movements at a more rapid pace. Without worrying about whether she had Mario's permission to yield to orgasm, she screamed immediately and her body writhed on the silky leather. The two men joined their wails to hers. Their compound cry slashed through the night, and dogs answered it in the distance with a chorus of endless barking. But they took no notice of it. They existed in another world. Their trio seemed to be regulated by an inner harmony, like the works of a watch. They had succeeded in forming a profound unity, without fissures, more perfect than any couple could have achieved. The *sam-lo*'s hands pressed Emmanuelle's breasts and she sobbed with pleasure, arching her back to let him enter her more deeply, panting that she was happier than she could stand and begging him to tear her, not to spare her, to come in her.

Mario sensed that the *sam-lo*'s endurance was inexhaustible, but he himself could hold back no longer. He sank his fingernails into his partner's flesh, as though giving him a signal. The two men ejaculated simultaneously, the *sam-lo* into the depths of Emmanuelle's body, feeling himself invaded at the same time by another outpouring. Emmanuelle screamed louder than she had ever screamed before, as the acrid taste of the semen that was inundating her rose in her throat. Her voice reverberated from the surface of the black water and no one could have said to whom her cry was addressed:

"I'm in love! I'm in love! I'm in love!"